TWISTED DELUSIONS

OJANd cole @ Gmail.com

By

Joe Noonkester

To Jane + Lynn T
Hope you enjoy!

PublishAmerica
Baltimore

ISBN: 1-60474-499-5
PUBLISHED BY PUBLISHAMERICA, LLLP
www.publishamerica.com
Baltimore

Printed in the United States of America

This novel is dedicated to my heroes, those police officers throughout the United States who on a daily basis place their lives in jeopardy for our safety and enjoyment. I applaud them and their families for the hardships they endure because of the profession they have chosen.

I especially want to acknowledge one of the finest police departments in the world, the Los Angeles Police Department, with whose training and experiences made this book possible.

ACKNOWLEDGMENTS

First and foremost, I want to thank my Lord and Savior, Jesus Christ, for his divine protection over the years, and for any ability that I might possess as an author. I give Him all the honor and glory.

Secondly, to my good friend Dr. Robert Carey for all the stimulating conversations we had relating to the complex world of psychiatry and its diagnosis and treatment. It was this phenomenon, the ability to probe the depths of the human mind and discover their reactions under certain pressures or stimuli that inspired me to write this novel. The seed was planted and cultivated and the character, Dr. Robert Forrest, began to emerge. Thus the novel, Twisted Delusions, was born.

Last but not least, I want to thank Bobbie Carey for her superb translation from English to her native French language.

Chapter One

He removed the orange juice from the cooler and was about to place it in his cart when out of the corner of his eye he saw his dead wife, a jolt of electrical current shot through his body causing his legs to buckle. The juice fell crashing onto the floor.

"Are you all right?" the woman asked, trying to help him regain his composure. Although she was not a nurse, she had sufficient medical training to believe something severe may have just occurred. The man was in a daze and was unable to focus his eyes, his skin was clammy and his gait was unsteady, and he had to hold onto his cart to keep from falling. Her mind flashed back in time when her favorite aunt suffered a mild stroke and she first learned of the three question test rule. The three questions would ascertain whether or not he was plagued with the same misfortune.

When he was able to catch his breath, he nodded meekly.

"Sir, do you know where you are?"

The man took a deep breath and nodded, his steel-gray eyes showing the effects of the trauma.

"Smile for me."

With much effort he gave a weak smile.

"Say something," she asked, this question being the most important of the three.

A puzzled expression came over the man's face, and then peace and contentment, "Thank you, my angel."

Donna flushed at his comment. "I think I'd see a doctor if I were you," she said turning to leave.

"Wait! Who are you and how can I thank you?"

Donna chuckled, "I'm your angel, remember? Thanks aren't required."

The man studied his new angel as she disappeared down the aisle. He didn't recognize her voice but her face was more than familiar; it was the same face that he had once courted, loved, and eventually married. But how could this be? She was dead! He knew this with certainty because he had caused her demise. He didn't know by what power she had come back into his life, but it defied all logic and explanation. Then the realization struck, she's returned to avenge her death; but just as quickly as the thought had surfaced, it was arrogantly shrugged off. "No, she still loves me," he reflected pretentiously.

The man kept Donna under surveillance until she entered the check-out line, and then he quickly filed in behind her. "I want to thank you for your assistance earlier," he commented.

A strange feeling crept up Donna's spine, warning her not to continue the conversation. She half-turned, giving the man only a quick glimpse, "It was nothing, but you should see a doctor."

The man noted the tone of her voice, "I don't mean to bother you, I only want you to know I'm all right."

Donna gathered her groceries without answering.

"Nice woman, that Mrs. Forrest," the man stated as the cashier began ringing up his groceries.

"You know Mrs. Forrest? I guess you would, since you and Robert are both doctors."

"Oh my yes, I've known Robert for many years but for some reason I cannot recall his wife's name."

"It's Donna."

"Donna…of course it is. How could I have forgotten?"

Two weeks later.

The rain came crashing onto the windshield of his car, lightly at first, then turning into a steady downpour. Reaching for the indicator switch, he light-heartedly hummed an old Irish ballad as he flipped the wipers on and they began dancing back and forth. It was now the wee hours of the morning and the Weather Channel had predicted more rain for the next twenty-four to forty-eight hours. The cold front had forced the temperature down to the mid-forties and the mild winds had turned to bone-chilling gusts, causing his car to veer dangerously as he fought to avoid the large puddles along the edge of the roadway.

Seeing headlights ahead, he slowed down and waited for the car to pass before making a left turn into Griffith Park. Once inside, he continued down the narrow road until he reached the central picnic area where he pulled to the curb. Protected from the elements, he took precious moments to survey every nook and cranny; the area contained no artificial lighting and appeared to be completely deserted. A bolt of lightening cracked in the distance sending a blinding flash of light across the skies, then just as quickly it returned to darkness.

When he was certain there were no witnesses, he opened the trunk as another bolt illuminated the lifeless form of a man lying inside.

Hearing movements, he turned with the quickness of a cat toward the noise and watched as a large German shepherd darted from the shadows and crossing the street only a few yards behind his car. A snarl formed on the man's face as he turned his cold steel gray eyes toward the darkness in search of the dog's owner and listened intently for any further noise. His mind returned to the business at hand as he watched the dog continue on its way.

He quickly reached inside and with powerful arms, lifted the man's body out of the trunk and onto his shoulders. He carried the body for several yards before dropping it onto the ground behind a wooden bench. Pausing, he took one last look around before finishing his task, a sadistic smile of satisfaction crossing his otherwise emotionless face.

"Oh my God."

"What's wrong?" Robert asked as Donna clutched the morning newspaper to her bosom.

"There's been another murder."

"Can I see?"

She tossed the paper on the table in front of her husband, "He's got to be stopped, Robert," she snapped.

Dr. Robert Forrest, one of southern California's leading psychiatrists and a partner in Forrest & Downey Associates, picked up the LA Times and began reading the headlines, *Fourth Murder in Two Weeks.*

He quickly scanned the article. *John Ferguson was found dead inside Griffith Park early this morning. The autopsy revealed death was caused by strangulation; this is the same Modus Operandi as the previous three killings. Police are setting up a special task force in the Hollywood Detective Division, headed by Captain Marcus Murdock, and are bringing in special homicide investigators from the entire Los Angeles area. Authorities are baffled as to the apparent motive and at this time have no suspects and are seeking any information about the crimes and its victims.*

Dr. Forrest gently laid the paper on the table and continued staring at its headlines as he methodically stroked his short reddish-blond beard, his mind automatically deciphering the evidence given.

He had previously assisted the police by compiling psychological profiles of various suspects, and his profiles along with those of other psychiatrists gave them a starting point as to what kind of demon they were looking for. In those previous cases, he had been amazingly accurate and in some instances was able to build a partial physical description of the suspect.

"What kind of a madman could do such a thing?" she asked.

"A very sick one, unfortunately the world is full of them. I think I'll call Joe Norris; if I'm going to be of any help I'll need to know a lot more than what the papers are telling."

"Oh no you don't; you're not getting involved in this one," she stated flatly.

"But if the public doesn't get involved, we'll never get such madmen off the streets."

"Not this one, Robert. Promise me?"

Although Robert was one of the most brilliant men she had ever known, she knew that like Sir Galahad, he would not rest until he had slain the dragon and saved the maiden in distress. If she had any chance of aborting his involvement, she had to put her foot down and do it now.

But for the moment at least, Robert looked anything but brilliant, sitting silently and pouting like a child that had just been scolded by his mother.

"Promise me," Donna pressed, but this time not in the form of a question but a command.

Robert smiled sheepishly, "Okay," he answered passively.

"Robert, I mean it."

"I said okay," he flinched.

Donna leaned down and kissed him on his forehead; "Now that we have that settled, can I get you some more coffee?"

Robert shook his head; "I've an early session with Donald this morning. I think we've finally gotten to the root of his problem and I feel it's time he has a little more space. He's a lot more relaxed and is now able to control his anxieties, but I'll be close by just to make sure."

"You seem to be more relaxed yourself lately, I know the things he went through really bothered you."

"I'm sorry, hon; I have to get inside his head to be of any help."

"I know, but lately I'm glad you're sessions with him are coming to an end."

Her comment caught Robert off guard. "Why do you say that? Hold that thought, I'm running late and really have to go. I'll call you later," he said picking up his briefcase.

His Mercedes convertible awaited him, the second love of his life. What passion he had for this grand car, and how he and Donna loved taking a leisurely drive along the coast with the top down, the wind blowing through their hair and smelling the crisp clean ocean air. Yes he was successful, and he took pride in knowing he had achieved it on his own through hard work and perseverance, with no extra baggage attached.

Even though he had promised, the killings consumed all thoughts as he drove toward his office on Century Boulevard in West Los Angeles.

Security Officer Miles Jordan was watching his television monitor as Robert put his card in the lock and the gate slide open.

"Good Morning, Dr. Forrest," he said cheerfully as Robert entered the building.

"Good morning, Miles; how was the week-end?"

"My wife and I had a great time. Thank you for the tickets, the play was great."

"You're quite welcome, I'm glad you enjoyed it," he replied stepping into the elevator.

There was no sensation of movement as it silently glided upward. When the door opened, Robert turned and headed toward Suite Five-0-Three.

Entering his office, he could hear the soft sounds of water emulating from the fountain; it was a subtle, relaxing, therapeutic sound, and one he loved and often used to set the mood when in a session with a patient. However, Donna thought other wise. She had a pesky fibroid tumor that needed to be checked every year, and to do so she had to drink and retain a ton of water before her lower ultra sound test could be given. And a so called, peaceful fountain was the last thing she needed to hear.

. Carol was at her desk going over paper work. "Good morning, and how's my favorite secretary?"

"Good morning, Doctor. You look as though you had a good weekend; did your sister-in-law fly down from San Francisco?"

"No," he reported sadly. "Something came up; she'll try next month."

"That's too bad; I know how you both looked forward to seeing her. Donald's in the waiting room and you have a message from Lt. Norris of the LAPD."

"Get the Lieutenant, and after I'm through send Donald in"

Robert sat down at his mahogany desk, his slim five foot eight inch frame looking lean but vibrant behind the massive wooden structure. He always kept himself physically fit and took pride in being in such great shape for a man in his mid-fifties. Even in college and graduating number one in the class of Nineteen Seventy-Nine at the University of San Francisco, he still found time to keep himself in shape by running, bike riding, and lifting weights. It didn't hurt his academics that his IQ was in the top two-percent, and that he was a member of the prestigious Mensa Society.

The red light began flashing, "Hello," he said picking up the phone.

"Dr. Forrest, Joe Norris."

"Hey Joe, my secretary said you had called."

"Yeah," Joe sighed. "Been reading the papers lately?"

"Unfortunately."

Listen Doc, I could really use your help on this one."

Robert ran a hand through his hair, thinking of the look on Donna's face when she begged him not to get involved. "I would if I could, Joe; problem is I'm really tied up with cases at the moment."

"I understand. Would you have time to look at a few photos and let me pick that genius brain of yours?

"I'd really like to help, it's just…" Robert scrambled for a better excuse but concluded, "This is really a bad time. Sorry."

"You got that right," Joe replied flatly. It's a bad time all over LA. Well thanks anyway."

"Tell you what," Robert interjected on a soaring feeling of guilt. "I really don't have time to get involved in this case, but if you can make it quick, I'll squeeze in a few minutes at One-thirty."

Robert's emotions were mixed, but he rationalized that merely answering a few questions was a far cry from getting involved. He closed his mind to the incident and opened the file lying on his desk.

Donald's history started with the accident in which he accidentally and fatally ran over a twelve year old boy that darted from between two parked cars and into his path. He had been under

Robert's care for the past fourteen months, complaining of nightmares in which he continually relived that dreadful night. The anxiety of knowing that he would be haunted in his dreams had kept him from sleeping to the point he was unable to function at work. His relationship with his wife was strained and he feared they would soon separate.

Robert then read the notes from his last session: Patient has not had any flashbacks of the occurrence in the past two weeks, and only occasionally in the past four. He feels he is in better control of his anxieties and of his guilt feelings; and his body language has changed dramatically from timid and scared to that of being more confident. He's asking to have more time between sessions.

Robert buzzed for Carol to send Donald in. He turned in his chair as the door opened, and with pen and notebook in hand he motioned for Donald to enter. Donald liked to sit on the couch facing Robert, and as usual he walked straight to the couch and sat down.

"How's it going?" Robert asked in a very business like tone.

"Very well, doctor."

"And how are you feeling today?"

"I'm feeling very good about myself; and as for the flashbacks, I haven't had any since our last session. Sometimes I think of my kids and what I would do if something like this should happen to one of them; and I think of the parents of that poor kid and my heart goes out to them. I don't think I can face them yet, but in time should that ever happen I think I could...as one parent would face another. I know it happened, and if I could change it I would. As we've discussed many times, it was an unfortunate accident but it wasn't my fault. I did everything I could to keep from hitting him, but he ran right in front of me and I just couldn't stop in time. The look of terror in the little boy's face will haunt me forever, and that's something I know I'll have to deal with. I wish it had never happened but it did...and it's really been tough."

Robert was amazed at what seemed to be a rehearsed speech from Donald. "These recurring flashbacks or nightmares have to be brought to the surface before any healing can occur. Sometimes we blame ourselves for things we have no control over. This is a big hurdle, and I believe you are now on the path to finally putting this behind you. How are things at home?"

"My wife and I are getting along great; and there's no more tension. She said she just couldn't stand by and see me going through this. I know she loves me, and knowing that helps a lot."

Robert listened intensely as Donald told of his feelings of work and other changes that were occurring in his life. As the session came to a close, Robert had one last question; "You mentioned in our last session that you would like to change our schedule. What do you have in mind?"

"Well," Donald said pausing as if trying to build up the courage to ask. "I was thinking of every two weeks."

Robert could see him holding his hands in his lap, his fingers crossed. "Okay, why don't we make it every other week? We can discuss it in our next session and see how it's going at that time."

"Thank you, doctor," his face beaming with happiness for the first time in months.

Robert stood up and extended his hand indicating the session was over, but instead Donald walked past Robert's extended hand and embraced him.

"Thank you so much, Doctor Forrest; I don't know how much longer I could have taken these guilty feelings. It's as though you've saved my life and I'm so grateful," he said straining to control his emotions.

Robert smiled, "Take care, Donald."

"I will," he promised.

Robert always kept his sessions purely professional, and it was during emotional times like these that made it difficult to stay within those tight guidelines. Donald opened the door and left with a noticeable spring in his gait.

Robert sat down and reopened Donald's file, smiling as he entered in his latest notes; 'Its times like these that I truly love what I'm doing, and to know that I have made life a little better for another human being, a father and a husband.'

Meanwhile, back at Hollywood Detective Division, Lieutenant Joe Norris is having a briefing with his detectives.

"Okay, any information on this guy, Ferguson?"

"Yeah Joe," Carter answered. "I interviewed the manager of his apartment; Ferguson was somewhat of a loner but did have a couple of friends that he hung around with. One, a guy called Angel, Hispanic, about thirty-five, five foot nine, one hundred-sixty-five pounds, he has long black hair and usually wears it in a ponytail. He's got a tattoo on his right shoulder with the name Angel and two crossed swords below it. The other guy's a male Caucasian, known only as Bob, thirty-five to forty with short brown hair. The manager's never gotten more than a quick glimpse of him."

"Thanks, Carter. Williams, run the name Angel through the alias files, if you come up with anything, put out an APB for information only."

"Okay, boss."

"Carter, what did you find in Ferguson's apartment?"

"Not much, it's a small one bedroom apartment with only the bare essentials. There was nothing of value inside, and the apartment didn't appear to have been ransacked. The lab will be sending photos as soon as they're developed."

"Slater! Brown!"

"Yeah, boss," Slater answered.

"What about the autopsy?"

"The autopsy was performed by Doctor Gucci; he concluded that the victim died of strangulation, just like all the others. The harp string was the murder weapon, but while he was still alive his tongue was torn from his mouth and his right hand cut off at the wrist and his stub shoved down his throat. Also like the others, his hand and tongue were not found at the scene. After he was dead; he was stabbed six times in the face, twice in the throat, and eight times in the chest. The victim's wounds match the wounds on all the previous victims and it appears to have been made by the same instrument. The depth of the wounds shows that the victim was struck with great force. Again, there were no marks or scratches to indicate a struggle of any kind, indicating that the victim might have known the suspect. Blood deposits were found on his back, the back of his arms, legs and buttocks; so he was lying on his back when he died. However, he was found facedown. His body had lost approximately two pints of blood but there wasn't that much at the scene, so it's obvious he wasn't killed at this location. We have photos of the scene and during the autopsy, and we should be getting them any time."

"Have you gotten a DNA report, and was blood found belonging to any other person?" Joe asked.

"All blood belonged to the victim," Slater continued. "We had Forensic go over his entire body and clothing, even his fingernails were scraped." Slater shook his head, "No foreign tissue was found, nothing, no where."

"Thanks guys," Joe said walking over to a large display hanging on the wall.

The display contained the pictures of the three previous victims, now a fourth would be added. How many more would hang before this maniac is caught, he pondered. There has to be a connection that ties the four together…some sick formula. The four did have some things in common; for one thing they were all males. Victim-One was a forty-five-year old Caucasian who sold new Chevrolets in downtown Los Angeles, and was one of their top salesmen. He had no record and was happily married with two grown children. He was friendly and out going, and had no known vices such as gambling or frequenting prostitutes. Victim-Two was a thirty-year old Caucasian selling real estate in Glendale. He was also a top producer, happily married with one small daughter, friendly and out going, and also with no known vices. Victim-Three was a sixty-year old Caucasian; a widower and a jeweler, but an introvert. He was financially healthy and also had no known vices. Victim-Four was a forty-five-year Caucasian who did odd jobs for a living, and an extreme introvert.

All victims worked in some type of sales capacity. Could the suspect have been the victim of a bad sales deal and now be stalking salesmen? Maybe meeting them through their work and building a relationship of trust, and then enticing them to some isolated area where he would do the killings?

Could that be why there was no struggle? But Joe's gut feelings said otherwise. So what was it? He scratched his head trying to put the pieces of the puzzle together. "Brown, have you talked to the coworkers of Victim-One or with any of the people listed in his personal sales log?"

"I've interviewed all of his coworkers; they haven't a clue why this happened. And I've talked to all of the people listed in his log; they were mostly married couples looking for a car, nothing out of the ordinary."

"Slater, what about Victim-Two?" Joe questioned.

"I've also talked to his coworkers; it's the same story, they were all shocked to hear what had happened. And likewise, his clients were mostly couples, none with the skills needed to butcher our victims in such a stylish manner."

"Had there been anyone hanging around the real estate office, an unhappy customer or anything of that nature?"

Slater shook his head, "Nope, nothing."

"Well keep looking; we have to find something to go on."

In a small dingy apartment on the forgotten side of town, a man is sitting alone on a worn out plaid couch. The room is in total darkness with the exception of one tiny lamp next to his head; his unshaven face etched deep with wrinkles and his worn out clothes telling of being too long on the wrong side of life. His life has been that of torment and his heart callused by too many days and nights alone. Alone to think of his past when all was bright and wonderful, when he had a beautiful wife and socialized with the rich and famous. Now he sits in his run-down apartment with no sunshine in his life to lift his spirit, and only the inevitable cockroach scampering by as a companion. He raises the newspaper to the light as his piercing steel-gray eyes strain to read its words. He presses his lips tightly when voices are heard in the hallway, and his cold lifeless eyes turn in their direction. The voices continue until they finally fade. When silence becomes the master, he raises the paper to study its headlines, *Fourth Murder in Two Weeks*. His lips begins to quiver, and in a vicious tantrum, he throws the paper on the couch and in one quick motion picks up a pair of scissors lying on the coffee table and maliciously thrusts the scissors into the heart of the article and deep into the couch.

"Wrong! Wrong! Wrong! Five dead bodies!" he grumbles loudly. "Are you such imbeciles that you can't find anything? How do you ever expect to find me? Number six will be easier to find, I promise you that."

He takes a deep breath as he tries to control his anger, and then calmly sits back down and methodically cuts the article from the paper as if never having been disturbed. He removes two thumbtacks from a small plastic tray and pins the clippings to the wall next to the three already hanging.

Robert hit the speed dial to Carol's desk, "When Lieutenant Norris gets here, please send him right in."

"He just came in." She turned to Joe, "You can go in now, Lieutenant."

Robert motioned for Joe to enter as he turned to face him.

"I appreciate your seeing me on such short notice, I have photos of the crime scene as well as the autopsy," Joe said pulling a packet from his suit pocket.

"They are not very pretty," Joe warned as they sat down on the sofa.

"I understand, go ahead."

"The first three photos are of Victim-One," he stated as he laid them side-by-side on the coffee table. The first is that of a male Caucasian, his left cheek is on the pavement, and it depicts the surrounding area. The next is a closer view; the third is a close-up showing the large puncture wounds on his neck and of the wire wrapped around his neck. "The coroner," Joe continued, "has determined that death was caused by the wire around the victim's neck, which is actually a harp string. The string is made by the D'Addario Company; they have been making musical strings for over two-hundred years. We've checked all stores in the area that carry the D'Addiario string, and apparently it is one of the more popular. This photo," Joe stated, "shows the victim's stump shoved inside his mouth. And this photo shows the victim's mouth being held open, revealing that his tongue had been ripped out. And the last one is a close up of the victim's bloody stump."

"Oh my God," Robert moaned.

Joe then spread out photos showing the victim lying on the examining table. He pointed to the wounds on his right cheek. "According to Dr. Gucci," Joe continued, "these were done after the fact, after he was dead. Now this is the gruesome part; all the victims' right hands were cut off and their tongues literally ripped out of their mouths while they were still alive."

"What?" Robert gasped.

Joe nodded, "That's right…while they were ALIVE! Dr. Gucci has also determined the knife used more closely resembles that of a scalpel used by surgeons to make the initial incision when in surgery."

Robert's thoughts intensified.

"If you'll notice how clean the victim's face and neck is? Traces of alcohol were found indicating all the wounds in the victim's face and neck area had been cleansed." Joe continued without waiting for Robert to respond. "Dr. Gucci examined the victim's right wrist and determined that the way the hand was removed…he called it disarticulation, and it is his opinion that it was done by a person with great knowledge and highly skilled in amputations…a person such as a surgeon."

"Are you saying that the person doing these macabre killings could be a doctor?"

"That's a strong possibly," Joe said raising an eyebrow. "We're not ruling anyone out."

Robert shook his head, "I'll have to think about this," he replied as beads of perspiration began appearing on his forehead.

Joe picked up the first photo again, "As you can see, this photo shows the victim's left cheek on the pavement and his chest and the top of his legs against the ground. Dr. Gucci found blood in the tissues of the victim's back and the back of his legs, indicating that when the victim died he was lying on his back. Clearly the victim was moved after he was killed."

"In other words, the victim was abducted and taken to a location where he was tortured, killed, and cleansed before being dropped off," Robert recapped.

"Exactly," Joe confirmed. "There's no evidence of any fight or struggle; so...A, the suspect either knew the victim...or B, the victim did not know the suspect was there until it was too late...or C, something was done to quickly immobilize the victim."

Joe then laid out the photos of Victim's Two, Three, and Four. "These are photos of the other victims." Joe flipped one of the photos over, "As usual, on the back of each photo is our investigation number as well as other pertinent information such as victim's name, date, time found, location found, race, age and etc."

"Okay," Robert responded.

"All of the victims died in the same manner. We don't know how he does it, but it's as though the victims just sits and allows him to butcher them."

Robert felt his jaws tighten and his stomach turn over, and he felt as though he was going to vomit.

"You look a little pale; are you all right?" Joe asked.

Robert wiped his clammy forehead with a handkerchief, "I'm okay; go ahead."

"I can't express how much we need your help on this case."

Robert nodded. "I know, but like I said earlier, I can't get involved."

"I understand; I only ask that you think about it." Joe then reached over and shook Robert's hand, "I know you'll do what's right, Bob."

Robert winced; a weak smile appearing on his face.

Chapter Two

The tension was heavy and one could feel the pressure being put on the detectives to solve this case, yet their actions had shown they were professionals. They worked in a systematic manner, focusing on any new information while investigating data already attained. They were like robots at their work, not letting humanistic feelings intervene. When information which looked like a real possibility fizzled, they were on to the next part of the puzzle trying to put each part in its place until there was something tangible to focus on. There were no playful antidotes to break their concentration, people were getting killed and their personal lives would wait until this maniac was captured and put behind bars. This was a time of no-nonsense, and they were all business.

For the magnitude of the case, this was a small unit and the phones were ringing off their hooks. The officers were trying to answer each call to the best of their ability, obtaining any information the caller might have and to reassure the ones that were just plain scared that this case would be solved. It was a horrendous task trying to sift through each call, making sure vital information was not being overlooked and yet not wasting valuable time on something that wasn't there. Weeding out the crank callers, psychics, and palm readers was extremely frustrating, while at the same time, trying to console the scared and the paranoid appeared impossible.

He wrapped his massive hand around the telephone, "Hollywood Homicide, Montahue."

"I have some information on the recent killings," the caller said in a calm but cold voice.

The hair on the back of Montahue's neck stood on end as if he unconsciously knew who the caller was, or maybe it was just the instinct a cop gets after years of working the streets. Montahue began waving his hands in the air and pointing to the telephone, all talking and movement ceased.

"What kind of information do you have?" he asked trying to remain as calm and collected as possible while adrenalin raced wildly throughout his system.

"Ha, ha, ha," the voice chuckled. "Who's in charge?"

"I'm a supervisor, maybe I can help you."

"You help me? You couldn't find your ass with both hands and you have the audacity to ask if you can help me? You're such an imbecile," he said in an irate tone, "but you can find a pen and paper can't you?"

"I can," Montahue replied, gritting his teeth because of the caller's sardonic comments.

"That's a good boy," the voice said sarcastically. "If you can find the Selma Hotel, and I'm not sure you can, there is something for you in apartment twelve." He then hung up.

"Ahh shit, that's him, I know it's him. Did we get a trace?"

"He hung up before we could nail it down," Slater answered.

"What did he say?" Joe asked.

"He has something for us at the Selma Hotel. I've never heard such a cold heartless voice. Did we get it on tape?"

"Brown, did you get it?" Joe asked.

"Just the last part," Brown replied.

"Slater, you and Williams go to the Selma Hotel and see what's there…and take a Black and White with you," Joe ordered.

Joe sat down on the top of Brown's desk as the other detectives gathered around. He was in a somber mood with nothing on his mind but what had just occurred. They listened to the recording until each word the man spoke was etched into their minds.

Joe sat silently, letting the information mull around in his mind and allowing time to focus on several possibilities. Then he turned to face the others; "This guy's killed four people, maybe more." Joe paused for a moment; "I have a gut feeling he's playing some sort of sick game, and if he is it can only mean more are going to die. He seems upset with us for not finding his victims sooner; but on a positive note, we now have a voice to go with his description. Brown, take the tape to the Lab. Have them check for any voice alterations and possible background noises. Look for anything that might tell us where the call was made. I want a copy ASAP."

Slater pulled the unmarked police car to the curb and a Black and White pulled in behind.

"We'll get the key, you two," Slater said pointing to the uniformed officers, "go to apartment twelve, do not knock or go inside. If anyone comes out, hold them, and for God's sake be careful! This could be a set-up."

Slater and Williams went to the manager's office and knocked on the door.

"Coming, coming," a female voice yelled from inside.

Slater and Williams flashed their badges, "Police officers, we need the key to apartment twelve."

"Why do you want the key? Did Mr. Dobson do something wrong?"

"No ma'am, but we do need the key and we need it now."

"Well you don't need to get huffy about it," she scowled as she opened a drawer and began shuffling through several key rings, "Here it is. This is the master, so don't lose it or I'll have to answer to the owner of the building."

"Thank you, ma'am," Slater replied, acting as though he didn't hear her snide remark.

Using the wall as a shield, Slater knocked on the door, "Police, open up!"

There was no answer.

He pounded harder, "Police, open up!"

There still was no answer.

Slater tried the doorknob, it was locked. He inserted the key and pushed the door open.

All was silent but a rotten stench emitted from the room. The smell was not new to Slater, he had smelled that smell many times over the years and he knew the problem had occurred several days prior.

"Aggg...whew," the uniformed officers gasped.

"We're going in, watch where you step and don't touch anything!"

Although it was a warm day, the heater was on and the heat only intensified the rancid smell.

Slater scrutinized every aspect of the apartment. The front room was tiny, and on the couch sat a pile of dirty clothing. Next to the clothes was a duffel bag containing laundry soap and bleach. The kitchenette was clean and everything seemed to be in its place. Although the bathroom door was closed, Slater knew where the appalling smell was coming from. He turned the doorknob and slowly pushed the door open.

"Oh shit," Williams groaned as he looked inside.

The shower door was closed, but a figure could be seen inside. Slater slowly opened the shower door exposing the body of a naked man, his body bloated to almost twice its normal size. The decaying process was well underway. A wire was wrapped around his neck so tightly; only the ends could be seen protruding. His face was twisted and frozen in fright. His eyes were decayed to the point they were unrecognizable. His right hand was severed and his stump was shoved inside his mouth. Blood was everywhere.

Williams tapped Slater on the shoulder.

"What is it?" he asked as he turned to face Williams.

Williams pointed to the sink and quickly left the room about to vomit.

"Oh my God," he gasped when he saw the man's tongue lying in a pool of dried blood.

Slater stepped from the bathroom, "Everyone outside, this is now a crime scene. You boys guard the front door and don't let anyone in."

While the uniformed officers secured the front door, Williams went to the manager's office to notify the Coroner, Photo Lab, and Prints. While there, he interviewed the manager as to whether the victim had any visitors the last few days. Then he notified Joe as to what had occurred, so Joe could determine whether or not he wanted to role on the call.

Slater used the time to scrutinize the area and mark any evidence before the specialized investigative units arrived. He moved cautiously and deliberately so as not to disturb even the slightest fragment. Once each piece of evidence was marked, the photo Lab and Latent Prints could begin their tasks. Then he began reconstructing the victim's last movements prior to the killing.

It was obvious the victim was intending to do laundry. But for some unknown reason, before leaving he took time to take a shower, or was taken into the shower. Either way, there was no physical evidence of a struggle. The killing had occurred several days prior, Slater surmised, due to the bloating and darkening of the victim's skin tissue. As the oxygen in the tissue dissolves, the tissue begins to deteriorate and becomes darker in color until it's almost black. The heat would cause the tissue to break down faster, thus causing a charred look sooner.

The victim was of average build but obviously still no match for the suspect. Did this mean the suspect was a large person with the ability to easily over power his victims? Or was he someone with special skills and knowledge, knowing exactly how and where to strike a fatal blow?

It appeared the victim died of strangulation, but it would be the Coroner who would ultimately determined the cause and approximate time of death.

The front door was locked and there were no signs of forced entry, did the victim know the suspect? If so, how well did he know him? Well enough for the victim to be taking a shower while the suspect was in his apartment? Were they more than friends? Or was he not aware the suspect was inside? If that was the case, because of the size of the apartment, the suspect would have to have gained entry after the victim stepped into the shower. If that was the case, did he have his own key?

Slater was tying to answer these nagging questions as well as determine what photos were needed when the photographer arrived.

"Oh shit, whew that's gross," the photographer gasped as he got a glimpse of the body. "This poor guy really got butchered, and he's been dead for a while I see," he winced. "You realize this stench will never come out of our clothes. I had a guy last week that had been dead for several days; I had to burn them…"

"Can we get to work, Randy," Slater interrupted. "I want photos of every room, including the couch containing the victim's laundry. I want shots from every angle in the bathroom. Get photos of the entire body and a close-up of the wire around his neck as well as the wounds on his face and chest area. Don't forget his tongue in the sink."

"Tongue?" Randy asked glancing over at the sink. "Oh my God," he gasped, turning a pale green.

"If you're going to lose it, Randy, do it outside," Slater remarked.

"Okay, okay…just give me a second," he sputtered as he began taking deep breaths.

"Breath through your nose, it'll help," Slater instructed.

Randy nodded and began doing as he was told. He had just about finished taking the photos Slater wanted when Joe arrived. Joe's eyes squinted as his nostrils caught the scent of the man's decaying flesh.

"He wasn't kidding; he's been butchered just like the others. The victim's in the shower. When Randy's finished, we can go in."

"Any ID on the victim?" Joe asked.

"His name is Robert Allen Dobson; he's a forty-five year old Caucasian. Williams is interviewing the manager."

"I'm finished, Slater," Randy called out as he exited the bathroom. "I hope you guys catch that son-of-a-bitch."

Slater nodded, "Let us know the minute you have copies."

"I'm on my way to the office now, and I'll see that you get a copy as soon as they're developed."

"Be sure and meet me at the Coroner's office, we'll need photos of the autopsy," Slater reminded.

"I'll be there, just let me know what time."

As soon as Randy had left, Joe and Slater cautiously entered the bathroom. Joe could see the victim's body slumped in the corner of the shower, his head resting against the tiled wall. Blood appeared to be intentionally smeared on the walls and shower door, but there was no specific pattern or message to be deciphered. On the shower floor was a large pool of dried blood, blood that had been pumped by a heart trying to fill an extremity that no longer existed.

Unlike the other murders, the suspect did not attempt to cleanse the area but rather, it appeared as if he had actually taken a shower after killing his victim. Could he have killed his victim and then taken the time to shower with the victim's mutilated body lying at his feet?

Joe was pondering these questions when Williams entered the room. "Any info from the manager?" he asked.

"Not much, but she did say he was always hanging around a guy named Angel. But she hasn't seen either of them for the past few days. Angel's Hispanic, five-seven, about one hundred-fifty pounds with a long black ponytail."

"Wasn't there an Angel hanging around Ferguson before he died?" Joe asked.

"Yes, there was," replied Slater.

At that moment a uniformed officer informed Slater that Latent Prints had arrived.

"I have to go; I'll be at Dr. Forrest's office if you need me."

Slater nodded and then turned to the latent print expert, "I want the whole apartment gone over with a fine toothed comb. There are a couple of items in particular I want printed. We'll start in the kitchen."

The front door opened again and the same uniformed officer stuck his head inside and announced that the coroner had arrived.

Joe approached Dr. Gucci as he entered. "I was just about to leave, but if you don't mind, I'd like a few words with you after you've examined the body."

"Sure thing, Joe, by the smell it shouldn't be long."

Dr. Gucci entered the bathroom, took one look at the victim's body and immediately pronounced him dead. He did a quick examination and then returned to the kitchen.

"I can't tell you exactly how long he's been dead until we get him to the lab, but it looks well past seventy-two hours," he said rubbing his nose.

"Thank you, Doctor," Slater replied.

Dr. Gucci then turned to Joe, "Did you want to ask me a question?"

"All our victims appear to have been killed without any signs of a struggle. Is there any conceivable way the suspect could make them just stand there and let him torture them?"

Dr. Gucci paused for a moment to ponder the question. "There are several ways. The human body has several pressure points that when pressed can cause a paralytic state, but the effect would not be long enough. It is more likely a drug is being used. There are drugs that can affect the nervous system, causing the victim to become momentarily paralyzed and thus not be able to defend ones self. One drug that readily comes to mind is, Curare. Curare comes from the bark of the Strychnos Toxifera or S.guianensis family; Loganiaceae and Menisperermacear Genus especially…"

"Hold on, Doc. Slow down." Joe interrupted. "What does that mean in layman terms?"

Dr. Gucci smiled, "So sorry. Curare is a potion used by the Huaorani Tribe, the most primitive in South America and occasionally by some of the other more remote and isolated tribes. They grind the bark and add poisons to the potion. Then they dip the tip of their darts into the poison and shoot their prey by blowing the dart through a small bamboo weed. Their prey becomes momentarily paralyzed and defenseless, yet they are left fully conscious. Some tribes during their voodoo practice use it because it is not a painkiller, therefore allowing the witch doctor to inflict whatever pain is desired. Some doctors here in the United States also use it in certain circumstances as an alternate form of consciously immobilizing their patients, but it is rarely used because the ingredients are hard to get and very expensive."

"Are you saying that it paralyzes its victim and leaves them conscious, but they can still feel the pain? Have you looked for any evidence of a drug of this nature being used in our victims?"

Dr. Gucci nodded, "Yes to both questions, but we haven't found anything at this point that would indicate a drug of this nature being used. However, used in the hands of a very skillful person it may never be detected, but we will continue to scrutinize our victims with this in mind."

"That could explain the frightened look on their faces. All the victims were stabbed several times, could the suspect be stabbing them to cover up a small puncture wound from a dart or a prick from a needle?"

"That's entirely possible," Dr. Gucci confirmed.

"How long would the drug have an effect on its victim?"

"That would depend on several factors," Dr. Gucci answered, "but mostly the potency of the drug. If the drug began to wear off before the desired time, he needs only to prick him again."

Joe paused for a moment, "I'll bet anything that's what's happening."

Joe stepped from the apartment and took a deep breath. "Damn, how many more are going to die before we find this lunatic?"

Joe couldn't stop thinking of the poor victim as he drove toward Robert's office.

"Hi, Carol, Dr. Forrest is expecting me."

"Hi, Lieutenant; yes, I know," she said sniffing the air.

Carol pushed the intercom button; "Lieutenant Norris is here."

"Send him in,"

Dr. Forrest was seated at his desk making some last minute entries when Joe entered.

"Thank you for seeing me on such short notice."

"You do remember me telling you that I'm not getting involved, don't you?"

Joe nodded sheepishly. He removed the cassette from his pocket and handed it to Robert.

"What's that repugnant smell?" Robert asked sniffing the air.

"We found number-Five," Joe replied looking somewhat embarrassed. "He'd been dead for awhile."

"That's terrible," Robert winced.

"Same MO," Joe countered. "We really need to catch this guy."

Robert acted as though he didn't hear Joe's comment. He placed the cassette inside the player and listened with ears trained to anatomize and decipher every word the suspect used. How he controlled the conversation, laughing one moment and lashing out the next, and then soft and tranquil as if never angered. Robert played the tape a total of three times, all the while taking notes.

"What do you think?" Joe asked when the tape had run its course.

"His voice is very cold, almost without feeling. He is aware of his actions and appears to be scolding the police...as a father would a child. One moment he's calm and in control, and the next he's outraged and cannot control his anger. His lack of control is a sign of Affect Disregulation. His choice of words and the way he controls the conversation is that of a very confident, articulate person. He thinks highly of himself and is usually in charge when dealing with people. These are the characteristics of a person with a Narcissistic Personality Disorder. Sometimes when a child is the victim of parental abuse, later in life, something happens that triggers those feelings or fears and brings them to the surface. He might start by having recurring dreams or nightmares, and then he places others such as in this case, the victims, in the position of the abusing parent and lashes out at them. In his own mind, he is getting back at the abusive parent for the pain and suffering they had caused. This type of abuse happens in every culture, rich or poor, no race is excluded. He could very well be a physician of some kind."

Joe looked amazed, "How can you tell all that?"

"It takes years of training, that's why they pay us the big bucks," he said with a sly grin.

"Now what?"

"Since all victims have all been males, and if the suspect was abused by a male as a child, it's more than likely he's reverting back to his role as the victim. In his mind he is getting even with his abuser, and in most cases like this, the abuser is most likely his father. If we're correct in assuming that, the cutting off of the victim's right hand might also be a symbol of the father's right hand, the one used to hurt him as a child. By removing the victim's right hand, he is removing the hand that abused him. And by removing the victim's tongue, the suspect might possibly be removing the cursing and brow beating he had received by his father."

Joe nodded, finally getting some insight on the illusive killer, "That could explain the motive. I really appreciate your listening to the tape, and if you think of anything else, please give me a call."

"As you know, I'm not getting involved," Robert re-emphasized.

"I understand. Thanks Bob."

Chapter Three

The temperature had fallen sharply and the weather quickly turned cold. It had been raining heavily all day, and although it had been reduced to only a light mist, its dampness penetrated your clothing sending a chill clear to the bone.

He sat in front of the television set with only an old blanket draped over his shoulders to keep warm. There was no piped in heat or thermostat to turn up, only a small electric heater a few inches from his feet, which didn't even take the chill out of the air. He sat glaring at the television and waiting impatiently for the evening news.

"Good evening, I'm Barry Snider and this is the Ten O'clock News. Our story tonight, the serial killer continues to strike fear and terror into the hearts of citizens in the Los Angeles area. And although it has been three weeks since the last killing, police are still no closer to solving the crimes. Doctor Robert Forrest, a leading psychiatrist in southern California, has stepped forward to join Captain Murdock's homicide team in an effort to help solve these senseless killings. Doctor Forrest has worked closely with the police on such matters and in the past has been accredited with narrowing the scope of investigation in several murder cases."

The man's tight lips turned to a sneer as they began showing excerpts from an interview taken earlier in the day of Mayor Walsh at City Hall introducing Captain Murdock and Doctor Robert Forrest.

His steel-gray eyes narrowed coldly as he methodically studied Dr. Forrest, etching his image permanently in his mind.

"Dr. Forrest," continued Barry Snider as the cameras returned to the newsroom, "has given the police a psychological profile of the killer, and will be working closely with Captain Murdock's team. Police are saying with his help, it's only a matter of time before the killer is brought to justice. On a more personal note, I only hope they catch this slimy piece of trash before anyone else is killed. And now we go to Ben Harper for the latest in sports."

"Thank you, Barry. The Los Angeles Lakers are…"

The man sprang from the couch and angrily turned off the television. "I know all about you, Dr. Forrest. You don't know who I am, but you will. So you've given the police a psychological profile of me, huh. Do you really think you can catch me? Do you really want to play this game with me? Let it be said, let it be done; I challenge you to a battle of wits. And as for you Barry Snider, Humpty Dumpty sat on a wall…Humpty Dumpty had a great fall."

That following Friday evening.

"Good evening Mr. Snider and Mrs. Snider you're looking lovely as always," the maitre d commented politely. "Welcome to the Oak Ridge Lodge, your table is ready."

"Thank you, William," Barry replied.

The Oak Ridge Lodge was a plush restaurant high on the fifteenth floor of the Harrington building. From its dining room, one could see the endless clusters of bright lights stretching from downtown Los Angeles all the way to Hollywood. It was an exclusive place where the rich and famous gathered to escape the prying eyes of the paparazzi and their star stricken fans. Each night its patrons headed a list of who's who in the world of entertainment and of the local political arena.

Barry scanned the room, waving to those he knew and to those who recognized him.

On the way to be seated, he passed Mayor Walsh's table.

"Sam, Marion, it's so nice to see you," he said shaking the Mayor's hand. "I hope you're enjoying your dinner."

"Thank you, Barry, we are," smiled Mrs. Walsh. She then turned to Gloria, "And how are you, my dear?"

"Things couldn't be better. I've been meaning to call you, I'm planning a birthday party for Barry in two weeks and I was hoping you might come."

"Honey, you know we'll be there."

"Thank you, Marion; I'll call you tomorrow," she said giving the Mayor a quick wink.

"Okay, dear; we'll talk tomorrow."

Barry Snider was head anchorman for the Ten O'clock News at KNXT television, and had been for the past five years. He was young, good-looking, intelligent, and enjoyed the recognition that came with being a well-known celebrity. He had earned his position through long hours of hard work, and those who worked with him liked and respected him.

The maitre d escorted the couple to a private booth next to the window overlooking the city of Los Angeles. The lights of the city shown bright and clear like dancing stars in the heavens.

"You'll enjoy the view from here, madam," the maitre d remarked as he pulled out her chair.

"Would you care for something before dinner?"

"Two Martinis, very dry," Barry ordered.

"Yes, sir," he replied, and quickly left.

"Oh, it feels so good to be with you. You've been working so hard lately, and I've missed you terribly," Gloria said squeezing Barry's hand.

"I know I've been neglecting you, but things are going to be different; the station has decided to give me the added help that I have been asking for."

"I'm so happy to hear that."

"Pardon me, Mr. Snider; but you have a phone call. You can take it in the lobby."

"Thank you, William. Would you order, I'll only be a minute."

"Please, don't be long," she pleaded.

35

Barry leaned down and gave her a gentle kiss, "I won't, I promise."

Barry hummed the notes to the soft music playing in the background as he nonchalantly walked to the lobby.

"This is Barry Snider," he said cheerfully.

"Hello, Barry; I have some very important information to give you regarding the serial killings."

"Who is this and what information do you have?"

"For my own safety I cannot divulge my name at this time, but I can give you the name of the person responsible."

"Who is it?" Barry asked.

"Ha, ha, ha," the caller chuckled. "It would be foolish of me to give you the information over the phone. I want to give it to you in person; it would be a great honor for me and a big feather in your cap if you cracked this case."

"When and where can I meet you?"

"It just so happens I'm also at the Oak Ridge Lodge. If you will meet me at the rear entrance in two minutes, I will give you his name. I even have photos of him."

"I can't see you now, my wife and I are having dinner."

"Then I'll just give the story to someone else. I must have been mistaken; I thought you were a top notch reporter. Good-bye."

"Wait, don't hang up. Give me a few minutes to let my wife know, and then I'll meet you."

"Ha, ha, ha," the caller chuckled. "No, no, no…if you want this story you'll have to come, right now! Your wife can wait a few minutes."

"You did say you have pictures?"

"Yes, I said I did. You have two minutes and then I leave!"

"Don't leave; I'm on my way."

Barry walked straight to a waiting elevator and descended to the first floor. He hurried to the rear exit and opened a door that led into a deserted alley. The area was extremely dark with only a single light shining over the back service door. He looked around; the area was cold, wet, and lifeless. A shiver ran up his back as his eyes caught the movement of a shadowy figure, when his eyes finally became accustomed to the darkness, the shadowy figure slowly transposed into that of a man.

"I'm Barry Snider," he yelled nervously. "Is that you?"

"Hello, Barry, I'm glad you could make it," the man said not moving from the shadows.

"Come out where I can see you," Barry replied, his voice cracking nervously.

"Would you like the information I promised?" the man asked reaching into his pocket and retrieving a small package.

"That's why I'm here."

"Then come on over, I don't want anyone seeing me giving you this," he coaxed, holding the package so Barry could see it.

"Who are you?" Barry asked as he stepped closer to the man.

"All the information you need is inside the package."

Barry eagerly reached out and grasped the package, and as he did he felt a sharp prick in his right index finger. He turned the package over and saw a small needle attached to its underside. Instantly, numbness spread throughout his body; he tried to turn and run but couldn't and fell to the ground. He tried to yell for help but nary a sound could he make. His heart pounded as if about to explode as the man kneeled down and pried the package from his hand.

"And now my pompous little king, come with me," the man said softly. "So cute, so successful...sitting on your decaying little throne, come for we have much to do."

The man picked Barry up and carried him to his car. He opened the trunk and dropped Barry inside as if he were the carcass of a deer poached out of season.

"Excuse me, William; have you seen my husband?" Gloria asked nervously.

"No madam, not since he got the phone call."

"It's been almost half an hour, would you see if he is still on the phone or in the restroom?"

"Yes, madam."

Gloria sat staring in the direction of the lobby, expecting to see Barry walking in at any moment.

She glanced at her watch, seven forty-five PM, it was the third time she had done so in the past ten minutes. He was now gone for exactly thirty-three minutes and Gloria could feel her anxieties mounting with each passing moment.

She saw William returning from the lobby at rapid pace. "You found him, is he still on the phone?"

"No, madam."

"Is he in the restroom?" she asked as she clasped her hands tightly together.

"He's not in the restroom, either," he replied with a worried look on his face.

"My God, where is he? What has happened to him? He wouldn't leave without telling me!"

Gloria stood up, her head in a daze and all sorts of uncertainties running through her mind.

She called out, "Barry, where are you?"

"Madam, please sit down."

"Oh William, where is he?"

"I don't know, madam," William replied as he assisted her into her chair.

"Gloria, what's wrong?" Mayor Walsh asked kneeling on one knee and taking her hand in an effort to comfort her.

Gloria turned to face the familiar voice, "Oh, Sam…something dreadful has happened to Barry, I just know it."

"Barry? Where is he?"

"He's gone!" she babbled.

"Gone, gone where?"

"I don't know. He got a phone call and never came back. He just disappeared."

"He's probably in the restroom. William, go see if Barry's in the restroom."

"I did, Mayor; he wasn't there. I've checked everywhere, he's not here!"

"How long has he been gone?"

"He got a phone call at exactly seven-twelve," Gloria replied, taking a handkerchief from her purse and wiping her nose.

"Maybe he had to go back to the studio," suggested the Mayor.

"He wouldn't do that without telling me. Something's wrong, I can feel it."

"Try to calm down. I'll call the studio myself. William," the Mayor said turning to the maitra' de, "get my wife and have her stay with Gloria. Then call the house doctor."

"Yes, Mayor."

Mayor Walsh picked up the telephone directory, thumbed through the yellow pages and found the number to KNXT Television.

"KNXT."

"This is Mayor Walsh, is Barry Snider there?"

"I'm sorry, Mayor Walsh, but Mr. Snider left hours ago. He'll be back tomorrow morning."

"Listen, I'm at the Oak Ridge Lodge with Mrs. Snider. Barry was here and received a phone call about an hour ago, and now we cannot find him. Did someone from the studio call, maybe an emergency or something of that nature?"

"No one here called. Did you say he's missing?"

"Let's just say that we cannot find him at the moment."

"Let me get this straight, he and Gloria were at the Oak Ridge Lodge, now he's gone and Gloria's still there?"

"That's right," replied the Mayor.

"Then something is very wrong. I know Barry and he would never leave Gloria like that. You'd better call the police."

"Yes, maybe you're right."

The Mayor stood for a moment not believing what had just happened, and not knowing quite what to do. He picked up the phone and dialed Nine-One-One.

Captain Murdock leaned back in his chair and began stretching his arms as a big yawn was being born. He like everyone else was putting in long hours of tedious work, trying to put a clueless jigsaw puzzle together. His eyes were burning from sorting through mounting piles of paperwork. He looked at his watch, twelve-thirty AM. He stood up and began stretching his aching back, "I'm getting too old for this kind of work," he muttered as he retrieved his hat and overcoat.

He stuck his head inside the detectives room, "Joe, it's time to go home; we both need to get some shut eye."

"You're right, Captain. I'll close up."

"See you in the morning," Murdock said as he closed the door.

"Good night, Captain."

Murdock made his way down the stairwell that led into the Hollywood Patrol Division, "Good night, Captain," said the night desk officer.

"Good night, son."

The air was crisp and he could feel the cold breeze penetrating his clothing as he stood at the top of the steps of the old police station gazing onto the street below. The heavy traffic had disappeared and the streets were now deserted. Stars were trying to peer through small openings in the thick black clouds, a strong weather front was quickly approaching and winter was well on its way.

He put his overcoat on and stuck his hands inside his pockets as he strode toward his car. The parking lot was now completely empty with the exception of his and Joe's. He hit the beeper unlocking his car, and half-asleep he climbed inside. He snapped his seat belt in place and began adjusting his rearview mirror when out of the corner of his eye he saw something that shot him back to alertness.

He let out a frightened scream as he grabbed his chest with one hand and frantically wrestled with the unyielding belt that held him captive with the other. "Oh my God," he gasped as he finely broke free, falling onto the pavement and rolling onto his back trying to catch his breath.

In the back seat sat the mutilated body of a dead man.

Chapter Four

We open our news broadcast tonight on a very tragic note; hello, I'm Troy George sitting in for Barry Snider. Last night our cities maniac murderer claimed his sixth victim; Barry Snider, our very own anchorman for KNXT Television was found early this morning brutally murdered. Barry's body was found by Captain Murdock shortly after mid-night in the Hollywood police parking lot...inside Captain Murdock's unmarked police car. Police have no clue as to how the body got there. The Sniders were having dinner at the Oak Ridge Lodge, along with many other celebrities including Mayor and Mrs. Walsh, when Mr. Snider received a telephone call at exactly seven-twelve PM, and was never seen again. We now go live to City Hall where Mayor Walsh, along with Chief of Police Tom Bradley, is holding a special news conference to answer some of the questions being asked by citizens regarding their safety."

Mayor Walsh and Chief Bradley are surrounded by journalists from every major newspaper and television station as well as the local radio stations clamoring to get their personal questions answered.

"Mayor, Mayor..." one voice could be heard above all the others, "Allen Wilson of the Los Angeles Times. As you know the city is in near panic; if this maniac can abduct a highly visible person such as Barry Snider, kill him, and then have the audacity to plant his body in the car belonging to the Captain in charge of the Special

Homicide Task Force, how in the world are police going to protect the average citizen?"

"Gentlemen, let's not try to create any more confusion than already exists. This has been a very embarrassing moment for our police department, especially for Captain Murdock and Chief Bradley. Let me assure you that we have one of the finest police departments in the nation; and now with the addition of Doctor Forrest, we have one of psychiatry's brightest minds helping us. Our police department has the complete backing of the Mayor's office and City Council. They have assured me that they are doing all…and let me reiterate…ALL they can to bring this killer to justice. Let's try to cooperate with them, let them do what they do best. And if we do that, I assure you this killer will be brought to justice."

"In this interview," Troy continued, "the Mayor is putting himself in a very precarious position, and if the police are unable to catch the one responsible, he just might be putting his own political career on the line. All of us here at KNXT are in shock, and wish to give Barry's wife, Gloria, our sincere condolence for her tragic loss…and we too share in her grief. Those who have worked with Barry over the years will miss his energetic smile and willingness to help. He was a good man, a gracious man, a man everyone loved and admired. His scruples were impeccable; and he made us proud to be a journalist…and we have truly lost a close friend. Barry would have been forty years old next week. This brings us to ask…just how safe are we? Can the police protect us from this madman? He seems to choose and kill at will. Now stay tuned as Ben Harper brings you the latest word in Sports."

"Turn that thing off," Joe snapped. "If anyone thinks they've been putting in long hours so far, they haven't seen anything yet! The heats on, and unless we catch this guy soon the temperature's going to get a lot hotter. Call your wives and tell them you won't be home for dinner; we have our backs against the wall and we're going to turn over every rock until we find him. The entire city's scared to death; the news media is hounding us for an arrest and our suspect's making a fool of us. Now with Barry Snider dead, every celebrity is calling and demanding special protection. No one feels safe and our citizens expect us to protect them; Hell, we can't even keep up with the phone calls that are flooding in. We have to find the missing piece that puts this puzzle together. Now let's get back to work and find it!"

Inside a large mansion nestled in a secluded area of the Hollywood hills, a lone figure watches Mayor Walsh's news conference on television.

"Yes, the city cries out like a young child being punished for his innocence. Like I was punished, so shall he. They're trying to rebel against me, but they don't realize that I too have been a victim. If they only knew how I was cheated out of my life and of my name, if they only knew!" A quick smirk crossed his lips, "So they think they can track me down like a wild animal, do they? Well the only clues they are going to find are the one's I want them to find. They don't realize who they are fencing with…me, the most brilliant mind they will ever encounter. I will toy with them like a father playing with his child; and I will hunt them like a great hunter hunts his prey. I will look into their souls; and then I will crush and devour them. Then I will take back my bride.

"Doctor Forrest's office, how may I help you?"

"I'd like to make an appointment to see Dr. Forrest."

"I'm sorry, but Dr. Forrest is completely filled and cannot take on any new patients at this time."

"This is Dr. Stanley Morgan; it would be greatly appreciated if I were able to speak with Dr. Forrest."

"Dr. Morgan, will you please hold?" Carol put Morgan on hold and buzzed Dr. Forrest, "Doctor, a Doctor Morgan is on line-one and wants to make an appointment with you. I told him your schedule was full and that you were unable to take on any new patients, but he insists on speaking with you."

"Thank you, Carol; I'll take care of it."

"Doctor Forrest, speaking."

"Doctor Forrest, this is Doctor Stanley Morgan; I would like very much to make an appointment to see you. I've been having these dreadful dreams and I've heard that you're the very best and I was hoping to talk to you about them."

"This is a little unusual, doctor; are you seeing another psychiatrist at this time?"

"No; but as one doctor to another, I have heard so many good things about you I was hoping I might see you," he reiterated.

"Are you in private practice, or are you working in one of the nearby hospitals?"

"I have my own private practice but I do all my surgeries out of St. Johns Hospital."

"My calendar is full but I did have a cancellation for Tuesday, if that would fit into your schedule, I could see you at ten AM on September third."

"That will be fine."

"Please hold while I transfer you to my secretary, and she will…"

Dr. Morgan interrupted, "I'll see you then, good-bye."

"Just a moment," Robert tried to interject but he heard a click and the phone went dead. "Of all the nerve, he hung up on me."

"Buzzz,"

"Doctor, your next appointment is here."

"Send him in; and keep my Tuesday cancellation free, I may have just filled it."

Donna stopped in front of the dairy case and removed a package of Mozzarella cheese, it was four-thirty and the store was bustling with people doing their last minute shopping before going home to prepare dinner.

Robert's partner and his wife were coming for dinner the following evening; Donna had originally planned a BBQ but she had found this fantastic Mexican recipe and all day she had been craving it with much anticipation. So at the last minute she decided to dash to the store and pick up the necessary ingredients to make this splendid dish and she had just enough time before Robert came home from work.

"Now let's see," she said rechecking each item in her cart, "I have the chicken, jumbo shrimp, cheese, Spanish rice, avocados, peppers, onions, sour cream, tomatoes, cilantro, lettuce, and the special enchilada sauce. I still need tequila and Triple Sec; how could I possibly forgotten the ingredients for the Margaritas?" she murmured to herself. "I must have walked right past them."

She made an abrupt turn about, crashing into the cart behind her, "I'm so sorry," she said apologizing to the man.

"That's okay; you do have cart insurance, right?"

Donna looked into his eyes, and although he was smiling it as though he were searching the depths of her soul. It was a strange uncomfortable feeling.

Without answering, she dashed to the liquor section, picked up a bottle of Tequila Gold and Triple Sec and headed for the cashier. As she was leaving the liquor section, the same man entered. Donna turned her head not wanting him to know that she had noticed, and quickly moved around an elderly couple that was stopped in the middle of the aisle.

When she felt she had lost him, she made a hasty retreat to the checkout stand and quickly began putting her items on the counter.

"Hi, how are you?" the cashier greeted as she began scanning Donna's items.

Donna took a deep breath, "It's been a long day."

"I hope you drive your car better than you drive your cart," she heard a voice say from behind.

Donna turned toward the voice, there he was again, this time the man's eyes were as piercing as a knife and his lips were shut tightly forming a quirky smile. Donna ignored his sarcastic comment, paid for her food and quickly left. She threw her groceries onto the front seat of her car and nervously scanned the parking lot; he was nowhere to be seen. She intentionally took the long way home, constantly looking in the rear view mirror to make sure she was not being followed. When she reached home, she hit the automatic garage door opener and drove inside.

"I'm so glad you're here," she said running into the kitchen and wrapping her arms around Robert's chest.

"You're trembling; what's wrong?"

"It's all these killings, you can't turn the television on without hearing how scared everyone is, and it's got my imagination working overtime. I stopped by the store to get some things for tomorrow night, and I bumped into a man's cart. The look in his eyes gave me the willies. I know its crazy but he scared me."

"You didn't drive straight home, did you?"

"No, no…I drove all over; I almost ran a red light making sure I wasn't being followed."

"Good girl; I want you to promise me that you'll be extra careful," Robert said giving her a kiss on the cheek.

Donna nodded, "Oh I forgot, I left the groceries in the car."

"I'll get them." Robert walked past Donna's car and opened the garage door to surveyed the area, there was no traffic and no one was in sight. He then closed the door and retrieved the groceries.

Parked a short distance away, he watches as Donna returns to the safety of her little nest. He looks at his watch knowing exactly how long it will take her to drive from the store to her house, and knowing she has taken an alternate route.

"Smart girl," he says in a soft low voice.

He waits a few moments and sees Robert come out of the house, do a quick surveillance of the street and then go back inside. He takes a deep breath as the feeling of power overwhelms him, and knowing they like the whole city are afraid. He grips his steering wheel as rage sweeps through his body, only after several moments is he able to regain his composure.

"I'll be back, and when I do I'll be taking my little angle with me," he promises as a smile crosses his face with the anticipation of what is yet to come.

Chapter Five

There was no emotion showing on the man's face, only a sly smirk that quickly disappeared as he opened the door.

Robert turned in his chair as Dr. Stanley Morgan entered. He was in his mid fifties, tall and distinguished looking with a muscular build; he had thick curly silver hair and was wearing an expensive double-breasted suit.

"How's it going?" Robert asked without getting up and even taking the time to retie one of his shoelaces.

Morgan stopped, his jaws tightening as he clenched his teeth. Anger began swelling deep within as he watched this petty little imbecile bending over and tying his shoelace when he should be on his feet greeting him. He doesn't realize who he's dealing with, certainly not one of his whacko patients that have lost control of reality.

When Robert finished tying his shoelace, he looked up having brief eye contact. Morgan's eyes were void of any sensitivity and his face was without expression.

Without saying a word, Morgan methodically scanned the room, etching every detail in his memory.

The room was plush but simply decorated, and one could hear the water fountain ever so slightly in the background. Against the wall to the left, was a light creamed colored leather couch with oak and glass end tables on either side and accented with antique brass lamps. Sitting in front of the couch was a matching coffee table with a large ceramic pot containing a beautiful Fuchsia plant, its bright lavender colored leaves and crisp white stamens glimmering in the sunlight that shown through a large picture window. Along the center wall sat Robert's desk with two oak file cabinets. On the wall to the right, sat an overstuffed recliner and beside the recliner sat a glass display case containing Robert's personal memorabilia, several pictures of him and Donna, and a ukulele.

Morgan casually strolled over and picked up the ukulele and began fingering the strings as only an expert would, then he began playing a chord from an old Irish classic, "Oh, Danny Boy."

Suddenly he stopped playing, "It's badly in need of being tuned," he remarked as he sat it down.

"You play very well; do you play any other instruments?"

Without answering, he walked over to the window and stood gazing at the busy world outside.

Robert watched, wondering what kind of person this Dr. Stanley Morgan might be.

Without turning from the window, he began speaking in a calm voice, "When I was a young boy, my mother and father would fight. I can remember being in bed and hearing my father coming home in a drunken stupor; my mother would plead with him to keep his voice down so that I wouldn't hear, but it only caused him to shout louder. "I don't care if that little bastard hears me or not!" Then I could hear him slapping my mother and her falling to the floor, crying. I was so afraid of him, and I would often hide under my covers when he came home. When I got older and after they fought, he would come into my room and beat me with his belt until my back and legs were bleeding. One night after they fought, I hid under my bed hoping he wouldn't find me. My father became so angry that he tore the covers off and threw them out the window. I can still remember the foul odor of alcohol on his breath as he reached under the bed trying to grab me, but I was too quick and slid to the other side. In a fit of rage, he ripped the mattress off and grabbed me around my neck; I couldn't breath and I thought he was going to kill me. He was so jealous of my superior intelligence; my mother knew I was special and tried to protect me, but she was only a woman. We were very close, so close that at times I felt as if we were one. Now after all these years, I've begun waking up at night, screaming and sweating profusely. I can still feel his hands wrapped around my neck and his fingers squeezing the life out of me; and I am terrified."

Morgan turned and faced Robert. "I think that's enough for now, I'll see you next week," he said as if dismissing Robert.

"Oh, okay," Robert replied, caught off guard with his abruptness. "I think that will be enough for today, but call me in a couple of days and I'll let you know the day and time of your next appointment."

Morgan's body stiffened as he raised one eyebrow in an allusive look, he then turned and arrogantly left without looking back.

"Whew," Robert gasped, leaning back in his chair and running his fingers through his hair, frustrated that for the first time in his career a patient completely dominated his session.

"Carol, did Dr. Morgan fill out the information form?"

"I gave it to him when he came in, but he's never returned it."

"The next time he comes in, make sure that he completes the form. Call Richard and tell him I'm ready for lunch."

Robert walked across the hall to Suite Five-O-Four.

"Good morning, Doctor Forrest; Doctor Downey is waiting for you in his office."

"Thank you, Shelly."

Robert entered, "Good morning, Richard."

"Hey Bob; would you mind terribly if we go to the restaurant across the street?"

"No, of course not."

Robert and Richard crossed the street and entered Leo's Coffee Shop, and sat down in a well-worn booth.

"Hi guys, coffee?" asked a tall slender waitress.

Robert and Richard both nodded.

"Today's special is Pastrami on Rye, or would you rather see a menu?"

"The special sounds good," they both agreed.

The waitress returned with a pot of coffee and poured each a cup.

Richard waited until she had left, "You're very quiet this morning, is everything okay?"

"The strangest thing just happen to me, it was really weird."

"Yes…and?"

"Well," Robert continued, "I had a new patient come in today, a doctor, and he told me the strangest story. It wasn't what he said that made it so strange, but the way he said it."

"What do you mean?" Richard asked, very intrigued by Robert's remarks.

Robert proceeded to tell Richard about Dr. Morgan and what had transpired.

"That's terrible!" Richard responded.

Robert began chuckling and running his fingers through his hair, "I know this is going to sound crazy, but this guy fits perfectly the profile that I just gave the police."

"Come on, Bob, that profile fits a lot of people."

"I know that, and I'm not suggesting that it's him at all, but if you could have seen the look in his eyes."

"Bob, as your partner and friend, I think you're getting a little too involved in this police stuff. You're one of the brightest psychiatrists I know, but you're not a very good policeman. You're not helping your patients and you're certainly not helping yourself. Stop it, get out and don't talk about it anymore, especially with Donna. You've done your part; now let the police do the rest. Anyway, didn't you promise Donna you weren't getting involved?"

"I did and I wasn't, but somehow I still got sucked in."

"And how's she taking it, now that you've been…sucked in?"

Robert winced, "Not very well, but don't try and change the subject. I know what I'm saying sounds strange," he said his frustration showing, "but you're not listening to what I'm saying. I'm not saying it's him; I'm just saying there's something very wrong with this guy."

"But I can tell by the look in your eyes, you do think it's him," Richard retorted. "Bob; you've just met the man, you don't know anything about him."

"I know I've just met him, but someone's butchering these people and if you knew the horrible things he's doing, you'd feel the same way."

"Probably, but I don't like seeing you getting this involved, and I hope you don't get paranoid with all your new patients."

"I'm not getting paranoid," Robert chuckled. "And I do realize that I know nothing about him, but this crazy thought keeps running through my mind."

"For Donna's sake, don't get involved any further."

Robert nodded, "You're right of course; you are coming over tonight?"

"That's a big, YES."

"Great; but let's keep this discussion between us."

"You can count on that!"

"Here you go guys," the waitress said sitting their plates in front of them. "Would you like more coffee?"

"Please," Richard replied.

"This reminds me of when we were in college, when either of us had a problem we would slip out, have a beer and talk about it. We were always there for one another other." He picked up his cup and took a drink, "Now we slip out and have coffee, we must be getting old."

They both chuckled.

"It was usually you with the problem," Robert continued. "And the problem usually involved a girl. I can still remember the night you met Shirley; you thought she was an angel. You two eloped after knowing each other only two months; remember, I was the one who told you that it would never work and that you should wait until after you graduate before getting married. I was afraid I would lose my best friend; but instead I gained another. You two married and were so happy…and I realized I was so wrong! After that, I began to have doubts about my having the ability to analyze and help people solve their problems; but after graduating and us setting up practice together, and me meeting and marrying Donna…well I just couldn't be happier."

"You had doubts about your abilities? You were only the top student at the university, but if I had your IQ I would have given you a run for your money," he said patting Robert on the arm.

"What I'm trying to say, is sometimes I see things so clearly and logically but I can still be wrong, like I was with you and Shirley. And I probably jumped to a conclusion with my new patient today too, but I'm glad we had the chance to talk it over because I do value your opinion."

"That's the Bob I know and love."

They finished lunch and walked back to their perspective office.

"I'll see you tonight," said a relieved Robert.

"We'll be there, and I'm happy you reconsidered your thoughts about this doctor. Ooo," Richard shuddered, "it would give me the willies to think I was alone in the same room with a killer,"

"I feel so silly," Robert thought as he entered his office. "Carol, get St. John's Hospital on the phone, I want to speak to Dr. Morgan."

In a matter of moments a voice answered. "St. John's Hospital, how may I help you?"

"This is Dr. Robert Forrest; I'd like to speak with Doctor Stanley Morgan, would you page him, please?"

"For future reference, Dr. Morgan's extension is four-thirty-three, hold while I transfer your call."

"Surgery, Nurse Kettle."

"Good afternoon; this is Doctor Robert Forrest, I'd like to speak with Dr. Morgan."

"I'm sorry but Doctor Morgan is not in at the moment. You're not the Doctor Robert Forrest that I've been seeing on all the news channels are you?"

"Yes, I guess I am. Tell me, has Dr. Morgan worked at St. John's long?"

"He's been here for several years, is something wrong?"

"No, no. I just need some information, that's all. What's his specialty at the hospital?"

"He's one of our most gifted and respected orthopedic surgeons," she boasted.

"An orthopedic surgeon, what type of surgeries does he perform?"

"He handles patients with severe injuries, usually when an amputation is required."

"Amputations?' Robert gasped.

"Yes, shall I have him call you?"

"I don't think that will necessary, but I do appreciate your help."

"Anytime, Doctor."

Robert's heart was pounding and his hands were trembling as he put the phone down. "Oh my God," he said, not believing what he had just heard.

Later that evening,

"Honey, would you get the door?" Donna asked as she continued tending the chicken enchiladas that were baking in the oven.

Robert opened the door, "Come in, come in," he greeted cheerfully, but inside he was still trembling and unsure of how to approach Richard with the news.

"Hi, there" Shirley said with a big smile as Robert gave her a light kiss on the cheek. "Donna's in the kitchen, why don't you join her."

"Yooo hooo," she cried out, scurrying toward the kitchen.

"Hello, good buddy," Robert greeted and giving Richard a hardy handshake. "I was just making some margaritas and I think you're going to need one," he remarked casually.

"Ahhh tonight is Mexican night, and a large frothy margarita with a little salt around the brim does sound delightful," Richard beamed.

"Come on," Robert said. "Let's join the girls."

Richard followed, and as Robert was pouring the margaritas, "What did you mean when you said, I'll need a big one?" he asked with a puzzled look on his face.

"Later," Robert smiled. "I've got something very intriguing to tell you, but first let's enjoy our drink."

"You sound very mysterious," Richard teased.

"I'll give the girls their drinks and we can relax in the front room."

After serving the girls, Robert picked up the remaining margaritas, "Here's to you, Richard."

"Thank you," Richard said with a suspicious look in his eye. He took a sip, "Ahhh, this is good, why haven't we had these before?"

Robert smiled, "Let's go in the front room where we can talk."

"Okay, now what's this intriguing news that I'm dying to hear?" Richard asked as he sat down on the sofa.

"I'm not quite sure how to begin, but remember our discussion about my doctor patient?"

"Come on, Bob, you're not back on that again are you? I thought we talked it over and it was all settled," his tone revealing his irritation.

"Well Richard; we did and it was," he said soberly. "So when I got back to my office I called the hospital where he resides; he wasn't there but the nurse said he had worked at the hospital for several years and was one of their most respected orthopedic surgeons."

"So you see," Richard interrupted, "it can't possibly be him. Come on, stop trying to be a detective, your patient can't be this…"

"Let me finish, Richard," Robert interrupted. "The nurse went on to say that he did most of the surgeries where people had been seriously injured and where an amputation was required."

"What?" Richard sputtered, almost spraying a mouth full of margarita.

After Richard regained his composure, "That still doesn't mean he's the one doing all these killings."

"No it doesn't, but if he is it's because he knows I'm helping the police and it could mean all our lives may be in danger. And you know what he's doing to his victims."

Richard leaned forward so the girls would not hear what he was about to say. "Stop it! You're scaring the Hell out of me and I don't want to hear anymore."

Robert continued as if not hearing Richard's request. "Remember when I told you about Donna bumping into a man's cart, and him scaring her so."

"Now what?" he asked sarcastically.

"She's never described the man to me, but if his description is the same as my patients, they could be the same person and if they are he could be stalking us. My patient is a male Caucasian, about sixty years old, six feet tall and well built; he has thick curly gray hair and piercing steel-gray eyes."

"Bob, that's pretty vague; there must be a thousand people matching that description, heck I even have gray eyes."

"Richard, please."

"Okay; if the two descriptions don't match that will be the end of it, right?" Richard demanded.

"Right," Robert replied, "and I hope to God they're not."

"Guys; dinner's ready."

"Coming," Richard quickly answered.

They gathered around the dining room table, the illumination from the crystal chandelier was set for a romantic evening, and Donna wanted everything to be perfect.

"Please, have a seat," she smiled.

They did, and Donna sat a generous portion of her yummy chicken enchiladas in front of each of them.

"That does smell good," Richard complimented as he leaned over absorbing its wonderful aroma.

"Would anyone care for another Margarita?" Robert asked.

Richard answered by waving his empty glass in the air.

"Can I get anyone anything before we eat?" Donna asked.

"No honey; please sit down," Shirley replied.

About half way through dinner, Robert casually asked, "Honey; remember the guy whose cart you bumped into while shopping; I was just curious, what did he look like?"

Donna turned to Shirley, "I didn't tell you what happened to me the other day, it was just awful."

"What happened, honey?" Shirley asked.

"I was picking up a few things for tonight's dinner when I realized I had forgotten the ingredients for the margaritas, when I turned around I bumped into a man's cart." Donna began chuckling; "He asked me if I had a cart license; of course he was only kidding and he was even smiling, but the look in his eyes scared me to death. It was like he was prying into my soul. Every time I turned around, there he was staring at me. I paid for my groceries and I got the Hell out of there," she said chuckling uneasy.

"What did he look like?" Robert asked.

"I don't know; nice enough looking I guess...tall, about sixty, but those eyes were like looking into death."

"What did his hair look like?" Robert continued.

"Let me think; he was wearing a baseball cap but what I could see was gray and curly."

"Anything else?"

Donna shook her head; "No; why are you asking?"

"Just curious," Robert answered, glancing over at Richard.

Richard began squirming uneasily, "Can I have another margarita?"

Robert retrieved the pitcher and refilled everyone's glass.

"Do you have plans for your anniversary?" Richard asked trying to change the subject.

"Yes honey; what are you going to do?" Shirley asked excitedly.

"Well, we've been thinking about going to Santa Barbara and getting a bungalow on the beach," Donna said smiling at Robert.

"Oh, you two are so romantic," Shirley purred clutching her bosom. "That sounds so nice. I know it's in October, but what day is it?"

"The first of October," replied a proud Robert.

"Have you made reservations anywhere?" Shirley quizzed.

"Not yet; why?" she asked.

"No reason. It's just that there's this lovely place that's right on the water, the Santa Barbara Resort, Richard and I just love it," Shirley cooed. "Each cottage has a cozy fireplace and a private

Jacuzzi secluded amongst the trees; it's like having your own Garden of Eden. I have the phone number if you'd like."

"That sounds great," beamed Robert. "Donna, why don't you call and make reservations?"

In the darkness of his elaborate mansion, he is watching and listening to every word that is being said. His jaws are clinched tightly and anger is mounting as he sees the love and happiness the two couples share.

"I'm the one who deserves to be happy, not that imbecile lover of yours," he fumes. "The Santa Barbara Resort, huh? Well, we'll just see about that."

Chapter Six

Donna lay gazing at the bedroom ceiling; slowly she turned toward Robert trying not to awaken him. His eyes were closed and a serene look was upon his face. She loved watching him sleep, and she was utterly content knowing he was there to comfort her in every conceivable way. She snuggled into her soft pillow, feeling so fortunate to be married to the man she loved and adored.

They were married twenty-five years ago come this Saturday, but it seemed like only yesterday that they had met, fell in love, and quickly married. Since that day her whole life evolved around him, and just the thought of him coming home from work each day excited her as though she couldn't wait. She still had that same tingling sensation she had that very first day. How lucky she was when several of her friends' marriage wound up in heartache and divorce courts.

"Twenty-five years," she sighed, slowly she grasped for her wedding ring.

In a flash she was sitting up in bed, her face white as a ghost, "Oh my God," she gasped.

"What's wrong?" Robert asked awaking from a deep sleep.

"My ring's gone!"

"What?" Robert asked as he tried clearing the numbness from his brain.

"My ring's gone," she repeated, raising her hand and showing Robert her naked finger.

Robert smiled, "You probably took it off when you showered."

"No, it's never been off my finger," she exclaimed.

Robert crawled out of bed, "I'll go get it, you probably left it on the sink."

Donna jumped from the bed, "If I did, I don't remember."

Although still half-asleep, Robert began searching the countertop. When it was not there, he got down on his knees and began searching the thick carpet in case it had fallen. But it wasn't on the floor either.

Meanwhile, Donna was pulling the covers off and searching the bed incase it slipped off her finger during the night, but it wasn't there either.

"When was the last time you saw it?"

"When I went to bed last night, I remember adjusting it on my finger."

"Did you get up during the night?"

She shook her head.

"I'll check the doors and windows, just to make sure everything's secure."

"Do you think someone might have stolen it?" she gasped.

"No, that's why I had this bullet proof alarm system installed, just to make sure that wouldn't happen," he assured her with a smile.

"Oh my God," she exhaled noisily. "It frightens me to think someone might be in our bedroom while we're sleeping."

Robert put his arms around her and held her close, "Nobody's been here, trust me. Why don't you fix some coffee while I a look around?"

Donna started to say something but reluctantly agreed to do as he asked.

He followed her downstairs, and while she went into the kitchen he checked the alarm system. It was still activated and seemed to be working properly. He checked the doors and windows, all were secure. Then a wineglass in the front room caught his eye. He picked it up and took a sniff. "Wine," he smiled. "No wonder she can't remember taking her ring off."

He held the wineglass behind his back and walked into the kitchen, Donna was at the counter cutting a grapefruit in half.

"The alarm system seems to be working, so you must have misplaced your ring. I'm sure you'll find it later." Then he held the wineglass out for Donna to see, "You must've gotten up and had a little nip after we went to bed," he said with a mischievous grin.

"What are you talking about, and where did you get that wineglass?"

"It was in the front room, it's yours isn't it?"

"No, it's not mine. You know we didn't have wine last night," she replied firmly.

"If it's not yours, then whose is it?"

"You tell me," she said walking over to the dishwasher and opening it, "There are the Margarita glasses we used last night."

Robert looked at the four-Margarita glasses, and then at the wineglass he was holding, "Then whose glass is this?"

Donna's lips began trembling as thoughts of the horrible murders surfaced. "Oh my God, someone was in our house," she said covering her mouth with her hand. "And I know my ring was on my finger when I went to bed. He must have taken it off while I was sleeping."

She wrapped her arms around herself trying to control her trembling.

Robert put his arms around her in an effort to console her, "Come on, honey. You're blowing this way out of proportion; no one was in our house. The alarm system is set and all the doors are still locked, no one could've possibly gotten into the house without setting it off," he said confidently, trying to reassure her...and himself.

"But my ring and that glass!"

"There has to be a logical explanation, you probably simply misplaced your ring. And I bet Richard or Shirley set the glass down and forgot about it. Yes, I'm sure that's probably what happened."

"I hope you're right, but I've got this strange feeling and it scares me."

"If it will make you feel better, I'll have the Alarm Company check the whole system. Not only that, but I'll have the glass fingerprinted. I'm sure we'll find Richard or Shirley's prints on it."

Donna gave Robert a gentle squeeze, "You're probably right, I just don't want to lose my wedding ring."

"You won't, we'll find it."

Robert placed the wineglass in a plastic baggie and sealed it. "Let's go have breakfast."

They ate without any further discussion; the events of the past evening consuming all of Robert's thoughts.

"When I get to the office, I'll call and give you the name of the person they will be sending. Don't let anyone else in, okay?"

Donna nodded, trying to force a smile.

"Stay and enjoy your coffee while I get my jacket," he said giving her a kiss. "I love you."

"Me too."

As Robert was removing his suit jacket from the closet, he noticed a dresser drawer open ever so slightly. A chill slithered up his back. He shook his head, scolding himself for being so paranoid.

"Good morning, Carol; I'll be making a couple of calls before seeing anyone. First, get me Joe Norris on the phone, and secondly, the Beverly Hills Security Alarms Company.

Robert went into his office and carefully laid the plastic baggie containing the wineglass on his desk.

He sat down and began stroking his beard while pondering the glass. The thought of anyone inside their house while he and his wife were sleeping terrified him, much less a killer. Would an intruder be so self-confident as to have a glass of wine while they slept? Then after foiling such an intricate alarm system be so careless as to leave his wineglass in such a conspicuous place, knowing it would be found and questions arise. Or was that what he wanted? Did he want the wineglass found, thus letting us know he could enter our house anytime he wanted? But could he really have gotten past my alarm system without setting it off? Am I blowing this way out of proportion, when the simple truth is Richard or Shirley simply left the wineglass?

Of course no one was in our house, he surmised. They were both alive, and if the killer had been inside, he and Donna would be dead now. Besides...

Robert was in such deep thought that when Carol buzzed, it startled him.

"This is, Lieutenant Norris, how may I help you?"

"Joe, this is Robert Forrest, I need to ask a favor."

"I'll do what I can."

"I know you're busy and I hope I'm not bothering you with something so trivial, but last night we had friends over for dinner. When Donna awoke this morning, her wedding ring was missing from her finger and she never takes it off. None of us had any wine, but I found an empty wineglass in the front room and a chair had been turned as if someone were sitting and looking out the front window."

"Where is the wineglass?"

"I put it inside a plastic baggie and brought it to work with me. I didn't want to talk to you in front of Donna; this whole thing has really frightened her."

"I'm sure it has, would you like me to stop by and pick it up?"

"You don't know how much I would appreciate your doing that, it will have my prints on it though."

"Just leave it with Carol. Is there anything else you need to talk to me about?"

"That's about it."

"I should be by in a couple of hours, and I'll get back to you as soon as I get the results."

"Thanks, Joe. Good-bye."

Robert buzzed Carol, "Get me the Beverly Hills Alarm Systems."

"Beverly Hills Alarm Systems, how may I help you?" a voice asked.

"This is Doctor Robert Forrest; I'd like to have someone check my alarm system. It seems to be working properly but I've had some unusual things happening."

"Let me pull your file, Doctor."

He entered his name in the computer, and Robert's file filled the screen.

"I see you have an XE Two-Forty security system. All your outside doors and windows are wired and you have a laser that will detect any sounds or movements within your house. If a problem is detected, a silent alarm will go directly to the Beverly Hills Police Department. Is your address of twelve-forty-six Arlington Way correct?"

"Yes."

"I'll send someone over as soon as possible."

"I appreciate that, however, with all that has been going on I'll need to know the name of the person coming and ask that he show identification to my wife when he gets there. I've instructed her to not let anyone else in."

"I understand. William J. Hodges will be the technician, and he shouldn't be long."

"Thank you, I'll notify my wife."

Robert immediately dialed his home number.

"Hi, it's me. The Alarm Company is sending a William J. Hodges, check his ID and don't let anyone in but him. Have him go over every inch in detail, I want everything working properly."

"Okay," she said nervously.

"Call me when he gets there, and call me when he leaves."

"I will," she replied.

"Oh, have you found your ring yet?"

"No, and I've searched the house from top to bottom. It's gone!" her frustration showing in the tone of her voice.

"Humph, darn. I have to go; I'll talk to you later."

Robert had been in session since nine AM and was anxious to find out what the Alarm Company had to say. He glanced at his watch, nine-fifty. "I think we'll stop for today," he concluded as he continued writing his notes.

"Okay, Doctor," Terry replied meekly. "I'll see you next week,"

As soon as Terry was gone, Robert buzzed Carol. "Were there any messages while I was in session?"

"Your wife called and said the man from the alarm company had arrived and that she would let you know the results. Also Lt. Norris picked up the wineglass, and Mr. Jenkins is here."

"I'll be making a call before sending Mr. Jenkins in."

Robert hit the speed dial, on the second ring Donna picked it up.

"It's me, is Mr. Hodges still there?"

"No, he just left and I was just about to call you."

"Well?"

"Everything's fine, he said everything is working exactly as it is supposed to."

"That's great, that's just what I needed to hear."

"Me too, I guess my imagination just went out of control," she chuckled.

"It's good to hear you laugh; I've missed that. I'll be home as soon as I can. I love you!"

"Love you too!"

My imagination's been running rampant too, he thought as his anxieties finally began to subside. "Send Mr. Jenkins in."

Jenkins entered the room and timidly sat down on the sofa.

"And how's everything going?"

"Well Doc, I'm still having these terrible dreams. I'm afraid to even close my eyes…"

One moment Robert's mind was intent on hearing what Jenkins was saying, and the next all his thoughts were of Dr. Morgan. He was so relieved to learn that it was impossible for anyone to enter his house without tripping the alarm. He could feel his face turning flush for ever having thought Morgan could have possibly been this fiendish killer. He could now put all this behind him and get on with his life.

Robert looked at his watch, not believing the session was almost over. He knew his mind had not been on Mr. Jenkins or of Mr. Jenkins' problems, but of his own personal tribulation. Richard was right, he was not a detective he was a doctor, let the police handle this murderer from here. I gave them the suspect's profile and now it's their turn to do what they do best.

My wife needs me and my patients need me, he thought as he leaned back in his chair watching Jenkins lips moving without hearing a sound.

Robert tried focusing on Jenkins but Morgan's face was all he could see. He glanced at his watch, eleven-fifty. "I think we can stop here."

"Thank you, Doctor. I feel so much better getting this off my chest."

Robert nodded, "I'll see you next week."

As soon as Jenkins had left, Robert was told Richard was in the office.

"Richard, what's up?" Robert asked.

"I just came by to wish you and Donna a happy anniversary."

"Well thank you, my friend."

"I know you're leaving in the morning, is there anything I can do while you're away?"

Robert shook his head, "You can find Donna's wedding ring."

"Oh no, she lost her ring?"

Robert shrugged, "It was on her finger when she went to bed, but it wasn't there when she woke up. But we did find an empty wineglass in the front room; do you remember whether you or Shirley had any wine last night?"

"No," he said shaking his head, "we only had margaritas."

"That's my recollection also. Donna must have gotten up during the night and had a glass of red wine, and for some reason took her ring off. That's the only explanation I can come up with. Our anniversary couldn't have come at a better time," Robert continued taking a deep breath. "And this trip is exactly what we both need, a chance to get out of Dodge, and with a little fresh air we'll be back to our old selves. Oh I almost forgot, I had the alarm company recheck our alarm system."

"And?"

"Everything's working perfectly," he smiled, shrugging his shoulders.

"And what about your new patient?" Richard asked with an impish grin.

"There are probably a lot of sixty-year men with curly silver hair."

"That's my, Bob. Welcome back!"

"Yes, Carol." Robert said picking up the phone. A short conversation ensued and Robert hit line two, "Hi, Joe."

"Bob, I just wanted you to know that other than yours there wasn't a single print on the wineglass. It appears to have been wiped clean. By the way, happy anniversary."

"Thank you, good-bye."

"That's strange," Robert said turning to Richard. "Other than mine, there wasn't a single print on the wineglass. Joe said it appeared to have been wiped clean. If Donna had been drinking from the glass, wouldn't you think her prints would be on it?"

"Bob, didn't you just tell me that it was impossible for anyone to get inside your house without tripping the alarm?"

Robert thought for a moment, "You're right, there has to be a logical explanation."

"That's right, now go and enjoy your anniversary."

Chapter Seven

It was a beautiful October day as Robert and Donna headed up the coastal highway, the convertible top was down and they could feel their anxieties disappearing with each mile that clicked by.

For an early autumn day, the sun was shining brightly without a cloud in the sky to spoil its deep royal blue color. The ocean seemed endless, extending mile after mile and only an occasional fishing boat or a sailboat dotting its horizon. The slight breeze was creating no more than a ripple effect on the oceans surface, and the sandy beaches below the rocky cliffs looked inviting as sun worshipers gathered to absorb the season's last rays. It was a gorgeous drive along this portion of the coast, and by mid day Santa Barbara could be seen nestled between the Pacific Ocean to the west and the Santa Ynez Mountains to the east.

It was revitalizing to shed their everyday hardships and responsibilities, to feel young again and explore what new treasures lie just beyond. They felt so alive and so very free!

They eagerly followed the instructions given them by Richard and Shirley and found their turn off without incident. They took the private driveway that led to a large knoll surrounded by cypress trees; in the middle of the knoll overlooking the ocean, sat the resort. It looked exactly as Richard and Shirley had described.

They could hardly wait as they headed toward the office. Inside was a large lobby and along one wall was a check-in counter with a young man and a very pretty woman busily helping customers.

"Good evening," the woman said as Robert stepped up to the counter.

"Hi, I'm Doctor Robert Forrest and I have reservations for this week-end."

She typed his name into the computer, "There are two in your party and you have requested the Honeymoon Cottage."

"Yes, that's right."

"Are you parked in the check-in area?"

"Yes, I am."

"Here's your key, Doctor Forrest. Teddy, please help Dr. and Mrs. Forrest to their cottage."

Teddy followed Robert to his car. "The Honeymoon Cottage is one of our more popular choices, and if you need anything just dial the desk."

Teddy led them down a narrow path, passing several cottages until they came to one sitting on top of a knoll amidst a cluster of trees. The cottage was surrounded by foliage, giving them all the privacy and seclusion they had hoped for. Donna squeezed Robert's hand with approval as they approached.

Teddy unlocked the front door. "Would you like your suitcases in the bedroom?"

"Please," Robert replied, picking Donna up and carrying her across the threshold like a strutting peacock in heat.

"Ooo," Donna cooed. "You still have it big boy," she said as he lowered her to the floor in an embrace.

Teddy gave them a moment to themselves, and when he returned Robert gave him a generous tip.

Donna marveled at the elegant room with its high vaulted ceiling, plush carpet and large comfy white suede sofa dotted with cushy pillows. Behind the sofa was a sliding glass door that led onto a balcony with an unobstructed view of the ocean. On the coffee table sat a beautiful flower arrangement and a bottle of champagne.

Donna removed the card. "This will be a weekend you will never forget,"

"Look Robert, those rascals sent us champagne and flowers, isn't that sweet," she said bending over and smelling their fresh sweet scent.

"Can I see?"

Donna handed Robert the card and watched him smiling as he read it.

"That's really nice," he said, his face showing the love for his friends. Then he began scrutinizing both sides of the card, "It doesn't say whom it's from, but Richard and Shirley are the only ones who know we're here. It's just like them to do something like this."

"This is going to be so nice. When we first talked about coming it seemed so expensive, but now that we're here, look at this room, its beautiful," she bubbled.

"Forget the cost, Mrs. Forrest, this is our twenty-fifth wedding anniversary and I want it to be one you'll never forget," he said as he wrapped his arms around her and gave her a slow sensuous kiss.

Donna responded by pulling Robert close.

He looked deep into her sparkling blue eyes, "Happy anniversary, I love you so much," he said with another kiss. "Let's see what the bedroom looks like," he said raising on eyebrow.

The bedroom was exceptional. It contained a king-size bed with ornate canopied brass posts, and in one corner was a lighted fireplace, its fire dancing to the rhythm of the soft music and filling the room with its subtle warmth.

Robert sat on the edge of the bed bouncing up and down like a kid with a new toy, "This is really comfortable."

Along one wall was a vanity with a large mirror, Robert flipped the switch and instantly dozens of lights flashed, lighting the entire area. Robert began making faces as he peered into the mirror.

Donna watched in amazement as the little boy emerged from within. "You're such a clown, no wonder I love you," she said walking into the bathroom and eyeing a large jetted bathtub sitting on a raised pedestal. The bathroom was completely mirrored.

"Wow! Robert come look at this."

"All right!" he boasted as he entered the room. "I'll be able to see you from every angle."

"Down boy, my angles aren't' as good as they were twenty-five years ago!"

"Let me be the judge of that!" he beamed.

"Well if you don't feed me soon, none of your fantasies are going to come true!"

He began singing and snapping his fingers, "What ever Lola wants, Lola gets." Then in a more serious note, "Richard says the French restaurant has dinners that are to die for."

"If we can eat without going to that extreme, I'm ready," she chuckled. "After dinner we can open the champagne, you never know this could be your lucky night;" she teased, a gleam now in her eye.

"You look ravishing, mademoiselle," complimented the maitre d in a heavy French accent as he nodded his approval of Donna in her black backless evening gown. "I am Francois, and Edwardo will be your waiter, will there be two for dinner?"

"Le bon soir, oui deux pour diner," smiled Robert.

"Ah Yvous parlez tres bon francaise, monsieur. S'il vous plait suivez-moi," complimented Francois.

"Merci. Ma femme est francaise et m'a tres bien appris."

Edwardo looked at Donna and smiled, "Et elle est belle aussi, votre femme."

"Merci," Robert replied. "Ce soir est notre vingt-cinquieme anniversaire."

"Les felicitations!"

"Merci," smiled Robert.

"Please, follow me," Edwardo said as he led them to an empty setting near the window overlooking the blue Pacific.

"May I, mademoiselle?" he asked as he pulled the black leather chair away from the thick beveled glass table.

"You may," Donna replied as she sat down.

"May I suggest our special for the evening, Fricassee de Mer et sa Julienne de legumes. It is wonderful!" he promised as he handed Donna and Robert their menu.

"Thank you; everything sounds so wonderful," she said looking over the menu. "Our friends agree, the Fricassee de Mer et sa Julienne de legumes dinner is exceptional," praised Donna.

"Thank you, mademoiselle. Will that be two?" he asked turning to Robert.

"Yes," Robert acknowledged.

"Would you care for something before dinner?"

"A bottle of white wine, extra dry."

"May I suggest, Vinoble Nineteen Eighty-Six French Chardonnay?"

"That would be an extremely good choice," Robert agreed.

"Merci," he said bowing his head courteously as he turned to leave.

"What a lovely place, and what a view," Donna cooed as they watched the sun slowly sinking behind the horizon, its brilliant colors of pinks and lavenders filling the skies.

In a matter of moments, Edwardo returned with a bottle of French Chardonnay, he opened it and poured Robert a glass for his approval. With a boyish grin, Robert gave the wine the Four-S-Test-sniff, swivel, suck, and swallow. "Excellent," he said happily.

"Merci," Edwardo replied filling their glasses.

Robert raised his glass in a toast, "To my beautiful Bride, whom I love more each day, Happy Anniversary."

A lone figure sits at a dimly lit table puffing on a cigarette, the smoke rising around his face as he casually blows perfect smoke rings into the air and watches as they slowly dissipate into oblivion.

He is a striking handsome specimen with a blond ponytail abutting his dark turtleneck sweater, the subtle light only accentuating the size of the golden medallion hanging around his neck as well as a matching golden bracelet on his right wrist, not to mention the Rolex on his left, shouting sinfully with his every move...look at me!

He lifts the double Scotch to his lips as he watches their every move, and a snarl forms on his lips as Robert leans over and gives Donna a loving kiss and of her response to his tenderness.

"Is everything all right?" the waiter asks when he sees the contorted look on the man's face.

He faces the waiter and his snarl turns to a sly grin as he speaks with a soothing calmness in his voice. "I was just thinking of an accident I had witnessed earlier."

The two men's eyes lock as he proceeds to describe the accident and all its grim details. A cold chill runs up the waiter's back as if an unknown force is probing the depths of his soul.

"Bring me another double Scotch;" the man snaps, breaking his spell over the waiter.

"Yyyes sir," the waiter replies nervously as he slowly backs away.

"For you, mademoiselle," and Edwardo presented Donna with the main course as only a suave Frenchman can.

"Oh my, this does look wonderful," she beams.

"Can I bring you anything else?" he asks as he presents Robert his.

"This will be fine, thank you," Robert replied.

It was Saturday night and the restaurant was filled with couples having a quiet dinner, but Robert's eyes could see only Donna. She was the love of his life and the only thing he wanted was to make her happy on this very special day.

"Would you care for dessert?" Edwardo asked as he began removing their dinner ware.

"Oh my goodness no, not me," Donna answered. "But dinner was every bit as delicious as our friends said it would be."

"Merci," he replied, placing a black leather folder in front of Robert. "If you're you a guest at the hotel, you need only add your room number and sign it."

Robert did, adding twenty percent to the amount.

They felt like two teenagers on their first date as they exited the restaurant arm in arm.

"Look, a falling star," Donna expressed with excitement as she pointed toward the heavens. They gazed as the star streaked brightly across the sky and then slowly began losing its glow until it faded out completely.

They strolled leisurely in the park-like setting, stopping occasionally for an intimate moment. When they finally reached their cottage, Robert drew Donna close and gave her a long sensuous kiss, neither of them noticing the footsteps lurking in the shadows only a short distance away.

"I want you so much," he whispered.

"Would you like to make it a threesome in the hot tub," she teased as she unbuttoned his shirt. "Just you...me...and our bottle of champagne?"

A sly grin emerged, "What will we wear?"

"Wear?" Donna questioned, disappearing into the bathroom and returning carrying two fluffy white towels. "Will these do?"

"Ooo," he cooed as he quickly removed the champagne from the refrigerator.

They doused the lights and slipped out of the cottage, dropping their towels as they stepped into the hot bubbly water.

From the shadows, their naked silhouettes were seen glimmering under a full moon.

How he hates them for causing the painful memories to resurface, memories of him finding his wife and her lover in their hot tub naked and embracing while in the act of making love. Their image permanently burned in his memory and the look of lust on her face as their bodies move slowly and rhythmically.

His jaws clench as the tension turns to excruciating pain, and he massages his temple in an effort to make the heartbreaking memories go away.

"They will pay for this," he promises.

"We're out of champagne," Robert said holding the bottle upside down and watching the last few drops fall.

"I'm ready for beddie by anyway, how about you?" she said rubbing his leg.

Robert was in such a relaxed state, he could do no more than grunt in agreement. They stepped from the hot tub, grabbed their towels and headed for their cottage.

Donna awoke not remembering when she had felt so alive. She whispered in Robert's ear that she was going to soak in the tub.

Robert murmured something unintelligible without leaving his unconscious state.

"Mmmuuhhh," she smacked, giving him a kiss on his cheek and then slipped out of bed. She went into the bathroom and turned the hot water on. When it was full, she slipped inside.

From another private cottage, Donna's every move is being scrutinized on his surveillance monitor, from the moment she awoke until she lay soaking in the hot bubbly water.

"Yes, my little mademoiselle, enjoy your bath, for your dreams will soon turn to nightmares. I will turn your world upside down and shake your very existence. Your life will have no meaning as Robert has made mine, and when I'm through you'll once again belong to me."

"Wake up, Robert," she said gently shaking his shoulder. "I'm starved, get dressed so we can go eat."

Robert rolled over but instead of getting up, he gently pulled her to him. "We could stay here and have breakfast in bed," he said nibbling her on the neck.

"You better save some of that for tonight," she teased, grabbing him by his beard.

"I give, I give," he laughed. "I'll be good."

Completely naked, he headed toward the bathroom.

"Not bad, buckaroo, are you available later?" she teased.

"Well ma'am, I don't rightly know. I got me a bunch of danged fillies to tame," he said in his best John Wayne imitation as he stepped bow-legged toward the bathroom.

Donna laughingly threw a towel; Robert made a quick side-step as it sailed past its intended target.

He shook his index finger as he retreated toward the bathroom, "Rule number one, ma'am, never throw at a naked buckaroo."

Donna chuckled, that was typical Robert; he should have been a comedian.

After he had reached the safety of the bathroom, Donna walked out onto the balcony; it was another beautiful California day and the sun was shining in all its glory. The surf was up and she could see the waves crashing against the rocks below causing the water to spew white foam. A little farther to her right was a white sandy beach with people frolicking along the water's edge.

She took a deep breath, filling her lungs with all of the oceans wonderful scents. When she could hold it now longer, she slowly exhaled until her lungs were completely exhausted. Then she went into her regular routine of stretching and bending until she could touch her torso to her legs.

In the midst of her routine, Robert opened the slider, "What time did the floor show start?"

"Oh, how I miss the ocean air and watching the birds soaring while looking for something to eat."

"Speaking of eating, are you ready?"

"I just need to comb my hair."

"I'll never understand, how can you improve the way you look right now? You look so happy and so vibrant!"

"I am happy, I can't remember feeling so free and so sexy." Donna smiled somewhat embarrassed but proud of her husband's ability to relate his feelings to her.

"Hmmm this looks good," Robert said biting into his blueberry bagel topped with heaping mounts of fluffy cream cheese.

Donna shook her head in disbelief as Robert nuzzled into his calorie soaked breakfast, "I'm surprised you still have any arteries left, with all the junk food you eat."

"I love this stuff. Besides the doctor checked my cholesterol and said I was in great shape for the shape I was in," he chuckled.

They sat in the shade of the umbrella as the warm sun caressed their skin, chatting and people watching as they strolled by.

"Have you ever noticed how different people are? I mean take a look at their face, it's only this big," he remarked holding his hands up and forming a circle only six inches apart. "They say everyone has a twin and there are multitudes of people who remind you of someone, but basically we're all different. It's truly amazing," he said shaking his head.

Donna shook her head, pondering how fast life was passing by. "It seems like such a long time since we've taken the time to just sit and enjoy each other's company." She squeezed Robert's hand, "I think we needed to get away from all the distractions and take the time to see what's really important in our life."

Robert leaned back and under the camouflage of his sunglasses, thanked Jesus for this wonderful woman.

Donna broke the silence, "Let's go to Sterns Wharf and spend the day just strolling around, and while you're paying for breakfast I'll go use the little girl's room."

As they were leisurely driving toward Sterns Wharf, they came across an old historical section of Santa Barbara. Donna was fascinated with the architecture and its adobe construction, but there were two she was especially fond of; one was built in Eighteen Twenty-Eight, Casa de la Guerra, located at Fifteen E. de la Guerra Street, and the other in Eighteen Seventeen, Casa Covarrubias, located at Seven Fifteen Santa Barbara Street.

After touring the area, Robert turned toward their destination, Sterns Wharf, a popular landmark in Santa Barbara that was built in Eighteen Seventy-Two to serve cargo and passenger ships. In the Nineteen Thirties, Sterns Wharf was used as a departure point for those wanting to board the nearby floating casinos. But today, it's a fascinating destination with many specialty shops in which to browse and excellent restaurants in which to satisfy even the most discriminating of patrons.

Robert found a parking spot, and he and Donna held hands as they headed toward the pier feeling like two college kids that had slipped away from school during lunch break.

They browsed every specialty shop, checking every T-shirts with Santa Barbara written on them as well as trying on every baseball cap Robert could find. Donna was in seventh-heaven when she found her favorite candy, home made chocolate fudge with walnuts. She purchased a pound as a gift for Richard and Shirley, and a piece for them to eat while strolling along the pier.

"Isn't that Joe and Colleen?" Donna asked, pointing to a couple walking down the pier.

"It sure is," Robert smiled. "Let's find out what they're doing here."

Robert and Donna hurried in their direction, "Joe, Cole," Robert yelled as he came within shouting distance.

Joe and Cole turned to face the voice.

"What are you two doing here?" Robert asked.

"Well if this isn't a pleasant surprise," Joe remarked, shaking Robert's hand. "We keep our sailboat here. I didn't' know you were coming to Santa Barbara for your anniversary."

"And I didn't know you were a sailor?" Robert retorted.

"Oh yes, we love sailing. Do you have time for a drink on the boat?" Colleen asked.

Robert and Donna looked at each other, "Do we, we'd love that."

"Great, come on." Colleen stated as they continued down the dock.

"I grew up in Santa Monica, I really miss the ocean," Donna stated taking a deep breath.

Colleen smiled, "You're kidding, I was born in Santa Monica. That's our boat there, she's sleek and very fast," Cole remarked proudly as if speaking of a member of the family.

"She's beautiful, what's her name?" Robert asked.

"Aquarius Sting" Colleen replied proudly.

"So one of you is an Aquarian and the other a Scorpio; that's neat. I've never been on a sailboat," Robert admitted.

"Robert, isn't there anything you can't figure out? I think you'd love sailing, it's so peaceful and quiet," Cole remarked.

"It does sound like a lot of fun," responded Donna.

Joe stepped onto the boat and sat down in the cockpit.

"Permission to come aboard, Captain," Robert asked, giving a quick salute.

"Permission granted."

Robert climbed aboard and stuck his head inside the companionway, "It's a lot bigger inside than it looks. Do you mind if I take a look below."

"Not at all. What would you like to drink, beer, red wine, or soda?" Cole asked.

"Wine," Robert replied, obviously enjoying the motion of the boat.

"I'll have the same," Donna and Joe answered.

"Would you care for some of Joe's famous guacamole?"

"Guacamole?" Robert asked.

"Robert loves Guacamole," Donna said with a smile.

"What are these instruments?" Robert asked with a curious look on his face.

"That's a GPS and the other is a Depth Finder, and knowing you, I'm sure you know what they are."

Robert smiled. "What kind of a boat is she?"

"A C&C, and she's a sloop."

"Sloop?" Robert asked with a bewildered look on his face.

A twinkle could be seen in Cole's eye. "A sloop has one mast while a ketch and a yawl have two. The difference between a ketch and a yawl is a ketch has its mizzenmast stepped in front of the rudderpost and a yawl has the mizzenmast stepped behind the rudderpost. On both a ketch and yawl, the front mast is taller while the front mast on a schooner is either shorter or of equal height. The Aquarius Sting has only one mast, so she's a sloop," Cole remarked, proud of her knowledge of sailboats and confident in her skills attained during many years of ocean sailing.

Robert was astonished, "I'm really impressed."

Cole poured the wine and handed them up to Joe along with the hors d' oeuvres.

They sat in the cockpit and listened as Joe told of his and Cole's plans of someday sailing south to the warm waters of Mexico; to frolic along its shoreline, snorkeling and scuba diving and to do it while they were still young and healthy.

The hours passed quickly and before they realized it, the sun was beginning to set.

"This has really been a treat, but I hope we didn't interfere with any plans you might of had," Robert apologized.

"No, no, we've enjoyed your company," Cole assured them, "and we'll have to go sailing one day."

Robert nodded, "We'd like that."

"We should be going," Donna reminded.

Robert extended his hand, "Thank you for such a memorable afternoon."

"You're welcome, compadre."

As they were getting into their car, Donna suggested they pick up some wine and slip into the hot tub before dinner.

Robert unlocked the front door, and before they reached the bedroom they were half-undressed.

"You know," he chuckled, "lately it seems we have our clothes off more than we have them on."

"Better enjoy it while you got it," Donna remarked as she slipped into her towel.

It was still early, but the sun was already shining brightly when Donna awoke. She could not help but notice the small package sitting on her nightstand near her head. She turned to her sleeping lover and gave him a light kiss trying not to awaken him, and then picked up the package and removed the card, "Happy Anniversary!"

She anxiously removed the wrapping and opened the small box inside, gasping and momentarily losing her breath when she saw its contents.

When she was finally able to control her emotions, she reached over and began shaking Robert. "Okay, why didn't you tell me?" she asked excitedly.

Robert rolled over and sat up, "Tell you what?"

"Don't play dumb with me, bucko" she said picking up a pillow and hitting him on the head with it.

"What are you talking about?" Robert asked while trying to avoid being hit by another flying pillow.

"What I'm talking about," she giggled, flinging the pillow several more times, "is why didn't you tell me you found my wedding ring? Where did you find it?"

Robert's jaw dropped, "What are you talking about?"

"My wedding ring!" she said, smiling and holding her hand so Robert could see that it was back on her finger where it belonged.

Robert's face turned as though he had seen a ghost.

Donna's smile vanished, "Stop it, Robert, you're scaring me. Please tell me you put my wedding ring in here," she said showing him the container."

Robert's face was void of expression.

Donna covered her mouth, "Oh my God," she gasped. "He put it there, didn't he?" Tears began rolling down her cheeks.

Robert pulled her close, "It's okay, everything's okay."

"Everything's not okay, what we are going to do?" she asked frantically.

"The first thing we have to do is stay calm. We have to think rationally. I don't think he wants to hurt us or he would have done it last night."

"I can't take it anymore, Robert, I'm too scared. This madman is stalking us and he's going to kill us!"

"No he's not, he only wants to scare us, can't you see that?"

"Well he's certainly doing a good job of it," she shot back. "Robert, I can't live like this. Let's get out of here, I can't stand being in this room, knowing he's been here."

"Okay, you pack while I go check out."

"Oh no you don't, you're not leaving me here alone."

Robert put his arms around her, "I'm sorry, you're right."

In a matter of moments, they were dressed and their suitcases packed. It was an entirely different feeling walking up the narrow path to the registration lobby. The dense foliage that grew along the edge way and provided them with seclusion from the outside world just twenty-four hours earlier, now meant possible dangers lying in wait in every nook and cranny along the way. Every tree and bush had a face, the face of a killer about to swoop down and devour them.

Chapter Eight

Dr. Rudolph Lucero opened the stainless steel door and pulled the bed out. The body was completely naked and the man's his right stump was shoved inside his mouth. His eyes are bulged and his colorless face frozen in terror. On his chest lay a business card, Dr. Robert Forrest, Psychiatrist. Written across the face of the card in blue ink was the name, Donald Madison.

"As I said over the phone, at approximately Ten-thirty I received a phone call from one of our janitors saying there was a corpse inside block One-Thirty-Three. Block One-Thirty-Three is listed as being empty, so I thought someone had merely put the corpse in the wrong slot. It's not a frequent mistake, but it does happen occasionally. Anyway, I came down to find out who it was and correct the problem. The moment I pulled the bed out I knew he was the victim of your serial killer. That's when I called you."

"Where's the janitor now?" Slater asked.

"I don't know. He was mopping the floor when I arrived, the next thing I knew he was gone. It was weird, he acted as though he knew me, but I had never seen him before. He wore a nametag, Jackson, so I didn't think much about it. We have so many employees and they come and go...you know what I mean."

"Would you page him? I have a couple of questions I'd like to ask."

"I knew you'd want to see him, so I asked the other janitors where I might find Mr. Jackson, but no one knew or had ever heard of him.

I became curious, so I checked the employee roster, but his name wasn't on it."

"What did Mr. Jackson look like?"

"He was African-American, about forty plus, six foot or so, approximately two-hundred pounds."

"Was there anything that might distinguish him from everyone else?"

Lucero shook his head.

"Do you have any idea how long the body might have been here?"

"It's hard to say. We have corpses coming and going, almost on a daily basis, although some have been here for as long as twenty years while we try to find their next of kin."

Lucero removed a three by five card attached to the door, "As a quick reference, the name of the corpse and date of arrival on this card. As you can see there's no name on this one, but for some reason there is a date."

He handed the card to Slater. "February fourteenth, that was almost seven weeks ago. Could the corpse have been here that long?"

Lucero shrugged his shoulders, "It's certainly possible."

It was a long quiet ride back to Beverly Hills, and although it was still warm, Donna was curled up in the front seat with her sweater pulled down over her legs and Robert was concentrating on what had happened and was trying to formulate a plan. He was in a confused state and didn't know which direction to turn. The more he pondered his situation, the less sense anything made. He had one of the finest alarms systems ever designed, and it was built by one the most respectable companies in the business along with all the bells and whistles money could buy, so how could anyone possibly get past it?

But the biggest question was how did Donna's wedding ring disappear from their home in Beverly Hills and then show up in

Santa Barbara. Everything pointed toward Dr. Morgan as being the culprit. But if he didn't do it, then who did?

The Alarm Company has to be wrong, that's the only explanation that puts things into an orderly perspective. And if they are wrong, then all the pieces of the puzzle would fit neatly into place. His mind was now set and it would take a lot of convincing to change it.

Robert pulled into his garage and closed the door, "Stay here until I check the house," he ordered.

He checked every conceivable point of entry, everything was locked and there were no signs of anyone having been inside.

He returned and helped Donna out of the car.

She was obviously nervous and confused, and afraid of being murdered in such a vicious manner. Relying on his vast knowledge and of his many years of being a psychiatrist, he took the time necessary to tenderly coax her from the car and into the house. After giving her nerves time to settle, Robert went into his office to call Joe while Donna busied herself preparing something to eat.

On the second ring, the phone was picked up. "Colleen, this is Robert Forrest, is Joe there?" he blurted.

"Robert, I'm so glad you called. Joe has been desperately trying to reach you. I don't know the details, but there was a homicide and he had to go back to Santa Barbara. He said it was imperative that he talk to you."

Robert's heart appeared to stop.

"And of course you know, Joe," Cole continued, "he wanted to see the crime scene and determine for himself if it was in fact the same suspect."

"That sounds like Joe."

"I'll call and let him know I've talked to you. Are you at home?"

"Yes, and tell him its imperative I talk to him."

Robert hung up the phone; he was a nervous wreck and was breaking out in a cold sweat. He went into the bathroom and looked into the mirror; his face was white as a ghost. He doused cold water on his face and watched as it cascaded down his beard.

"What am I going to do? I can't tell Donna what happened in Santa Barbara, and what could Joe possibly want?" He splashed more water onto his face and then dried off. His face was still blanched, so he tried patting it in hopes of bringing back some color.

As he approached the kitchen, he noted the concerned look in Donna's eyes, "You look so pale," she said stroking his cheek.

"It's probably from not eating," he lied.

"I heated some leftovers, I hope you don't mind?"

They ate without saying a word, and although the atmosphere was tense, Robert knew what steps must be taken. The hard part was bringing it up without scaring Donna any further.

"I was thinking," Robert spoke breaking the silence. "It's been a while since you've seen your sister, have you thought of visiting her?"

"Not without you, I haven't," she quipped.

"Don't you think this would be a good time for you two to get together?"

"Robert, is something going on that I don't know?"

Robert shook his head, "I would just feel better if you weren't here right now."

"Robert, what's going on," she said cutting through the chase.

Robert took a deep breath, knowing he was cornered and that she would not let up until he had confessed. Then as if a prayer was being answered the phone began shouting for attention, "That must be, Joe. I'll be right back." Robert hastened into his office and picked up the phone.

"Bob, thank God I've found you...."

"Colleen mentioned there was a homicide in Santa Barbara, and it might be our suspect," Robert interrupted.

"Yes there was, and he is. It occurred on the beach near the Santa Barbara Resort."

"Santa Barbara Resort?" Robert gasped.

"Yes, it's an upper class resort..."

"I know," Robert interrupted impatiently. "That's where we were staying."

"What!"

"And that's not all; remember me telling you about Donna losing her wedding ring? Well," Robert paused, "Sunday morning Donna found it. It was inside our cottage."

Joe's voice became very serious, "Listen to me very carefully; you and Donna are in grave danger."

"I know, but I think he's just trying to scare us. If he wanted to kill us he could have done it a number of times."

"Bob, something has happened that you aren't aware of. Do you know who Donald Madison is?"

"He's a patient of mine, why?"

"He was a patient, Bob. Slater called me right after you and Donna left our boat. Donald Madison's body was found inside the LA County Morgue. His wife has identified his body. They say he'd been dead for approximately six weeks."

"That's impossible; I've been having sessions with him every other week. I was with him just yesterday."

"No Bob, you weren't."

"Are you suggesting I've been seeing the serial killer?"

"That's exactly what I'm saying. Get Donna out of there, now?"

"I can send her to her sister's in San Francisco," he answered almost in a panic.

"Why don't you do that? A Black and White is on the way to spend the night, and they'll be dropping off a police radio in case there's any trouble. We'll talk further tomorrow."

Robert returned to the kitchen. "Donna, we've got to talk. Apparently there was a murder in Santa Barbara while we were there, and Donald Madison is dead."

"Santa Barbara? Donald dead?" she asked as a flurry of possibilities raced though her mind. "Oh my God; he is stalking us, isn't he?"

"It looks that way. And to be on the safe side, tomorrow you're going to visit your sister."

"I'm not leaving you, not when you need me."

"Hon, if you're at your sister's I won't be worrying about you."

Donna paused, "Do you really want me to leave? I don't want you to be by yourself."

"Shhh," he said putting his finger to her lips. "Everything's going to be fine. Joe's sending a Black and White over with a police radio so we will have immediate communication."

At that moment, the doorbell rang, "That must be the police."

"Oh God," Donna sputtered, her heart sinking to new lows.

"Honey, they're merely dropping off a police radio, that's all," he said trying to calm her.

But to be cautious, Robert peered through the peephole to make sure it was them. "Good evening, Officers," he said as he opened the door.

"Good evening, Dr. Forrest. Lieutenant Norris asked us to drop this radio off. If you need us for any reason, turn this button to the On position and then push this button to talk," he said giving Robert instructions how to use the radio. "We'll be close by to make sure nothing happens."

"Thank you, good night."

"Good night, Doctor."

Donna's flight from LAX was scheduled for eight-thirty AM, and her sister was to meet her in San Francisco.

Robert and Donna tossed and turned all night. Donna out of frustration for having to leave but too frightened to stay, and Robert because he was doing something he never dreamed he would be doing, sending Donna away because he was unable to protect her. He had never felt so helpless.

The traffic at the airport was extremely busy, and the only available spot to park was in an unloading zone. From there they walked to the United Airlines ticket counter, and after showing sufficient identification, Donna was given her boarding ticket.

Donna's flight was about to depart, but instead of boarding she flung her arms around Robert's neck in an embrace, "Please, be careful," she pleaded.

Robert held her tightly, "You won't be gone long," he whispered.

"I'm going for one reason and one reason only," she said with a stern look. "So you won't be worrying about me. This man's dangerous and I don't want anything on your mind except catching him."

"You don't know how much it means your saying that. I'll be careful I promise."

"You better, I don't know what I'd do if something should happen to you," she said proudly.

She gave him one last kiss before leaving.

Robert waited until her plane was completely out of sight before slowly turning toward his car. He was nauseous and missed her already!

"St. John's Hospital."

"Extension four-three-three, please."

"One moment," the voice said, and Robert could hear his call being transferred.

"Surgery, Nurse Kettle."

"This is Doctor Robert Forrest; I'd like to speak with Dr. Morgan."

"Dr. Morgan won't be in today."

"Humph," Robert said thinking this might be a good time to get information. "I tried contacting Dr. Morgan over the weekend but I couldn't reach him, would you happen to know if he's been out of town?"

"I've got his schedule right here, Doctor. It says he was on Call all weekend and performed emergency surgery early Sunday morning. I can have him call you tomorrow morning if you'd like."

"That would be fine, he has my number."

"Damn," he said putting the phone down. "If he was on Call all week-end and even had emergency surgery Sunday morning, then there's no way he could have possibly been in Santa Barbara. Then who returned Donna's ring? Who else knew where we were staying?" The more he pondered the question, the more confused he became.

"I have a friend who was an eye-witness to one of the serial killings," the voice on the phone said.

Slater raised his arm briskly, everyone stopped what they were doing and a hush fell over the room. Brown started recording the call.

"Who am I speaking with, and what information do you have?"

"Let's just say that I'm a Good Samaritan," he said in a soft calm voice, "and I want to help you find this vicious killer."

"What information do you have?"

"A friend told me he and a pal went to visit a man in his apartment, and while they were conversing in the bedroom someone knocked on the front door. The man went to answer it, leaving the bedroom door ajar."

"And what is your friend's name?"

"Everyone calls him Angel, but his real name is Juan Martinez."

"And what was Angel's friend's name?

"John Ferguson."

"And the person whose apartment they were at?"

"His last name is Dobson; I don't know what his first name is."

"Keep him on the line," Joe whispered.

Slater nodded, "Then what happened?"

"The man apparently did something to Dobson because they saw his head jerk backward and then he seemed to freeze. The man picked Dobson up and carried him into the bathroom and closed the door. While they were inside, Fergie tip toed over and peered through the peep hole. Suddenly the door burst open and Angel could see Dobson sitting on a chair, his face was full of blood and the man was holding Dobson's tongue in his hand."

"Then what happened?"

"The man threw Dobson's tongue into the sink and started chasing after Fergie. Angel said he was so scared he caught the next bus to San Diego."

"Do you know where we might find him?"

"He called and gave me his address, and he said he was never coming back."

"What is the address?"

"The Wilson Apartments, Apartment G, I hope this information help's you in some way."

"We'll check it out, is there a number where we can contact you?"

"Click," and then there was silence.

Slater looked up at Joe, "He hung up."

"Good going, Slater," Joe said patting him on the back. "Carter, did you get the location?"

"It was from a pay phone on the north/west corner of Hollywood and Vine."

"Well that's not going to do us any good." Joe turned to Slater; "This is your baby, call the San Diego PD and tell them he's a material witness in a murder case. Have them pick him up and let us know us as soon as they do. You and Brown, bring him back." Joe turned to Brown, "Victim-Six, wasn't his name Dobson?"

"Robert Allen Dobson."

"That connects Victims Four and Five. We now know why Ferguson was killed; the poor bastard was in the wrong place at the wrong time. But why was Dobson killed? Now if San Diego PD can find this guy, it just might be the break we've been hoping for."

"Hey, how did you like the Santa Barbara Resort?" Richard asked as he entered Robert's office.

"It was beautiful, and I want to thank you for the champagne and flowers."

"Champagne and flowers? What're you talking about?"

"Didn't you send champagne and flowers?"

"No," he replied shaking his head. "It would have been a nice gesture, but no I didn't."

"Well somebody did, it seems we have a lot to talk about."

They entered the same small restaurant across the street, found an empty booth and sat down.

The waitress placed a menu in front of them, "Coffee?"

They both nodded.

"Our special today is a BLT meal with a bowl of hot bean soup."

"Hummm, that sounds good," Richard replied.

"Make it two," agreed Robert.

"Two specials coming up and I'll be right back with your coffee."

"You're acting strangely, are you okay?"

"I've got a big problem," Robert announced. "I had to send Donna to her sister's."

"Are you two having problems?"

"Much worse."

"What do you mean much worse? What could be worse than that?" Richard shot back.

"Like her well being for example."

"You're talking in riddles, what do you mean, her well being?"

"Here you go," the waitress interrupted.

Robert waited until she had left. "Do you remember me telling you about Donna losing her wedding ring?'

"Yes, but what does that have to do with anything?"

"Well, we found it!"

"That's great, but don't sound so depressed about it"

"You don't understand, Richard, Donna's ring was taken off her finger at our house."

"Wait a minute," he interrupted. "I thought you said she took it off and forgot where she put it,"

"Let me finish, Richard. The morning of our anniversary, Donna woke up and found a present on her nightstand, thinking it was from me she opened it. Inside was her wedding ring!"

"And you didn't put it there?"

"No I didn't, but that's not all, when we arrived there were champagne and flowers waiting for us. We thought you and Shirley had sent them. It's now obvious that someone other than the four of us knew where we were going to be staying, but he even knew which cottage."

"Bob, I can't believe this is happening."

"Well Richard it is, and I haven't even told you the worst."

"The worst?"

Robert nodded, "Someone was murdered while we were there."

"Murdered!" Richard gasped.

"Yes and Lieutenant Norris went to Santa Barbara and confirmed our killer is the suspect. It turns out," he said pausing to take a deep breath, "that it happened right on the beach where we were staying."

"Holy Moses, what are you going to do?"

Robert shook his head, "Dr. Morgan can't be the suspect, because when I got back I called his hospital, he'd been on call all weekend and even performed emergency surgery Sunday morning. No, it's not him and I have no idea who it might be."

Richard chose his words very carefully, "Whoever is doing this has taken a special interest in you, and not to be sounding ungrateful but this guy's a butchering killer, why is he doing all this…and not killing you?"

Robert shook his head, "I've wondered the same thing, it's as if he wants to scare us to death."

"Joe, Slater's on line-one."

Joe waved, indicating he had heard, "Go ahead, Slater."

"Joe, I just talked to our witness and he's in real bad shape. San Diego PD had him locked in an interrogation room. When I first saw him, he was crouched in the corner like a scared child trying to hide."

"Is he the same Angel we're looking for?"

"Yep, he's got a tattoo of Angel and two crossed swords on his right shoulder. It's definitely him."

"What did he see?"

"He saw exactly what our caller said he saw, and that's what puzzles me."

"Why should that puzzle you?"

"He asked how we knew he was there and I told him a friend of his was worried about him. He said he only had two friends, Dobb and Fergie, and they were both probably dead. He said when the suspect chased Fergie from Dobb's apartment, he was so scared he didn't stop to talk to anyone, he just left town as fast as he could. I told him we would protect him but he's scared shitless about coming back to Hollywood. "

"And you feel he's telling the truth?"

"Oh yeah, and you would too if you saw the terror in his eye's…well Joe, you know what he saw."

"Yeah, well be careful, we don't know what this guy will do next."

"We'll be leaving in a few minutes and we should be there in a couple of hours."

Joe hung up the phone and then dialed Robert. "Bob, I was hoping you might stop by the office for a little while?"

"What's going on?"

Joe leaned back in his chair, "Something very interesting has just occurred, we received a phone call from a man telling us where we might find a witness to one of the murders. Slater and Brown went to San Diego to pick him up. There should only be four people that know what happened in the victim's apartment, the two victims and they're both dead, the witness we're picking up, and the murderer. Now it seems we have a fifth; and our witness claims he didn't say anything to anyone. So that could mean our caller and the murderer are the same person. And since the murderer seems to be stalking you, I was hoping you might listen to the recording and see if his voice sounds familiar, or at least give us some insight."

Robert took a sip of coffee, "I'm eating, but I'll be over as soon as I finish."

"I didn't mean to interrupt your dinner; take your time, it will be a couple of hours before Slater and Brown get back anyway."

"This is Johnson at the front desk; Dr. Forrest is here to see Lieutenant Norris."

"Send him in." Montahue turned to Joe, "Lieutenant, Doctor Forrest is here."

"Come on in, Bob. Would you like a cup of coffee while we listen to the tape?"

"Please."

After giving Robert his coffee, they listened attentively trying to pick up some overlooked clue. Although the voice was unfamiliar, for some unknown reason Robert still unconsciously compared it to that of Dr. Morgan. But it was obviously not Morgan, his choice of words and how he used them was different, and he lacked the sinister undertone.

When the tape had run its course, Robert shook his head, "It doesn't sound familiar."

"I've sent copies of both recordings to SID, I should know tomorrow if they are the same person." Joe looked at his watch, "I don't understand what's taking Slater and Brown so long, they should have been here by now," he said sounding like an old hen when one of her chicks strays too far from her side.

Joe was sitting with his legs propped up on his desk telling Robert of the time he and Colleen were sailing and found themselves battling a big storm when the door opened and Slater and Brown escorted Angel inside.

"What's the possibility of all four of our tires going flat at the same time?" Slater asked with a disgusted look on his face.

"What?" Joe gasped.

"Yeah, somebody let the air out of all four of our tires."

"It's him, I know it's him and he's going to kill me just like he killed Dobb and Fergie," Angel sniveled in a heavy Mexican accent. "You gotta protect me, you promised."

"Have a seat Angel. We said we'd take care of you and we will." Joe said sternly but passionately. "But in order to do that, we need to find out what this guy looks like."

"He's crazy man, he ripped Dobb's tongue right out of his mouth and now he wants to do the same to me!"

Joe placed his hand on Angel's shoulder, "Calm down, no one's going to hurt you. I'm going to ask you some questions and I want you to answer them the best you can. Had you ever seen this man before?"

Angel shook his head, "No man, I'd never seen him before."

"Can you describe him?"

"Oh I can describe him; I see his face right now. I always see his face. I see his face before I go to sleep and I see his face when I wake up. He's big, at least six feet, and those eyes, the way they look at you…he's crazy, man!"

"Okay, now relax. Is he White, Black, or…"

"He's White, man," he blurted, "and he has a scraggily beard."

"How old do you think he is?"

Angel shrugged, "I don't know man, it's hard to tell, his skin had lots of wrinkles…maybe sixty."

"What color is his hair?"

"Brown, long stringy brown hair, he's going to kill me man, I know it."

"No he's not, because we're not going to let him. Was there anything unusual about him, any scars or tattoos or anything that would set him apart from everyone else?"

"No man, just those eyes…like they were looking into your soul. He's real weird, man."

"What color are his eyes?"

"I don't know, man," Angel said shaking his head. "I just saw all that blood and I panicked."

"What kind of clothing was he wearing?"

"Dark, man."

"Was he wearing any special type of clothing, like those of a doctor or medical personnel?"

"No way man, more like somebody living on the streets, kind a dirty looking."

"And you say you saw him rip Mr. Dobson's tongue out."

"I didn't say that, man. I said that when he opened the door he already had Dobb's tongue in his hand,"

Angel's whole body began trembling as he described what he had seen. "Dobb just sat there, but I could tell he was still alive because I could see his eyes moving…and he was crying. The man threw Dobb's tongue in the sink and chased Fergie out of the apartment."

"And Mr. Dobson was sitting in a chair when the man chased Mr. Ferguson out the apartment?" Joe asked.

"Yeah man, he was just sitting there."

"Did you try to help Mr. Dobson?"

Angel shook his head, "There was no way that I was going in there. I didn't know when he was coming back."

"What did you do after he chased Mr. Ferguson?"

"I climbed out the window, man…and I ran like Hell until I couldn't run no more. That's when I decided to go to San Diego, so I caught a bus."

"Why did you choose San Diego?"

"I grew up in San Diego, other than Mexico, San Diego and Los Angeles are the only places I've ever lived."

"Does the killer know where you live?"

"I don't know man; I don't know what Dobb or Fergie might have told him."

"Sergeant Slater and Sergeant Brown are going to take your statements, and then they'll take you where you'll be safe. Tomorrow you'll meet with an SID expert, and by using a special technique he'll be able to put together a composite of the man you saw. You're a brave man and I want to thank you for your help," Joe said extending his hand.

Angel grabbed Joe's hand, "Please, don't let him kill me, man."

Joe shook his head, "Don't worry."

"Brown, take Angel's statements while Slater arranges a place for him to stay."

After they had left…

"Well Bob, what do you think?"

"Angel's obviously terrified and is in Post Trauma Shock. He saw something horrible, and it's going to take a lot of therapy before he recovers."

"I think you're right, and I want you to be careful, too," Joe warned.

Chapter Nine

Donna awoke from a restless night's sleep, and although she was comfortable, it always took a few days to get used to a new bed. Even as a child, her mother compared her to the princess who could feel the pea under her mattress.

Feeling foreign weight on her stomach, she reached down to push it aside when she recognized it to be Connie's Siamese cat. "Is my little pussycat cold? Would you like to snuggle?" she asked in a child like voice and lifting the cat and nuzzling her face into its soft fur. Donna lay half-asleep stroking the cat when it dawned on her that the cat was neither moving nor purring. She slowly lifted the cat and watched as its head fell limply to one side, its tongue dangling from its mouth.

Donna shot to alertness, screaming hysterically and flinging the cat from her arms.

A second wave of horror struck when she became aware of something wrapped tightly around and cutting into her neck. Seeing blood, she lost what little control she had and jumped from the bed, curling her body into a ball like a frightened child.

Connie came bursting into the room, "Donna, what's wrong? What's the matter? Oh my God, what are you doing?" she asked when she saw her sister crouched in the corner and bleeding from the neck.

Donna was beside herself, she was like a caged animal looking for a means of escape.

"Jimmy quick, I need your help," she screamed.

Her husband came rushing into the bedroom.

"What's happening, did she try to kill herself?" Jim asked as he began scrutinizing Donna more closely.

"Jimmy," she scolded. "Help me hold her!"

Jim wrapped his arms around Donna's trembling body as Connie began removing the wire.

"It's okay, honey, it's all right," Connie kept repeating. "We have to get this off."

Donna was incoherent, she couldn't catch her breath nor could she stop screaming. Then the warm liquid began running down her leg and forming a puddle at her feet.

"Oh honey, you poor dear," Connie stated as she try and comfort her younger sister.

When she was finally able to remove the wire, she took the bedspread and wrapped it around her trembling sister.

"Jimmy, call an ambulance."

"Your patient is here, Doctor."

Morgan glared arrogantly at Carol, "Your patient?" he thought as he opened the door and stepped inside.

Robert turned in his chair to face Morgan and even stood up to greet him, he wasn't sure why he did this, because he had never done it before. Was it because he was so relieved to learn that Morgan couldn't possibly be the heinous murderer? Or was it his way of merely showing one's respect to a very brilliant doctor?

"Shall we get started?" Robert asked.

As if ignoring him, Morgan walked directly to the display case containing Robert's personal memorabilia and picked up a picture of him and Donna, "Is this your wife?"

"It is."

"You both look very happy," he said softly as a mischievous grin began to form.

Robert felt uneasy about his comment and his reason for saying it. "You seem to be very curious about my personal life," he said resting his chin on his hand and studying Morgan's reactions.

Morgan put the picture down and walked over to the window and began peering out, "The sound of the water is very therapeutic."

"The sound pleases you in some way, Doctor Morgan?"

"It's very calming and soothing…like a woman's touch," he responded.

"And what woman comes to mind when you think of calming and soothing?"

"My mother was both calming and soothing and deserved much better," he replied without looking toward Robert.

"How so?"

"I would wake up in the middle of the night, and my father would be beating her and calling her filthy degrading names."

"What was that like for you?"

"She was a good woman and didn't deserve to be treated that way, she realized how special I was and was grateful that I was her son."

"What were your feelings toward your father?"

"My father was very strict, and he felt everyone should do as he said, if not they deserved to be punished. He was a harsh man and his words cut like a knife. I tried to make him proud of me but he wanted me to be a mirror of himself, but I wanted to be me."

"So you struggled to be other than a mere reflection of your father, huh?" Robert asked.

"Me? A mere reflection?" he responded, his eyes shooting daggers.

"You seem to resent the implication as if it belittles you or something, can you tell me more about your reaction?"

"He knew I had a brilliant mind and was musically gifted, but he thought that was for sissies, so out of jealousy he prodded me toward manlier aspirations." he revealed disdainfully. "I admit, I was an outstanding baseball player, and because of it our school went to the League Championship for three consecutive years, and winning two championships mainly due to my hitting and fielding prowess but even that wasn't enough. After I had conquered baseball, he turned his eyes toward football! But it didn't matter whether it was baseball or football; I was still an outstanding athlete. I made the UCLA Varsity Team roster in my freshman year and by the time I was a senior I was voted the Most Outstanding and Most Valuable Player, having rushed for more yards in the school's history than any other player. Every NFL team was scouting me, but my father demanded that I sign with the Los Angeles Rams. Not because they were our home team but because they were his favorite. During this time I also became a black belt in Karate and participated in several tournaments in which I never lost a bout. And I did all this while maintaining the highest grade point average in the history of UCLA."

"That's very impressive, and did you sign with the Rams?"

"As great as I was, I knew it was my mind where I really excelled."

"Buzzz. Buzzz."

"Carol I'm still in session."

"I'm sorry, Doctor, but you'd better come quick."

"Please excuse me, I'll be right back," Robert apologized.

Morgan nodded, a fiendish smile creeping across his face.

"You better take this," Carol stated handing Robert the phone.

"This is Dr. Forrest."

"Thank God I found you, something terrible has happened."

"Connie, what's wrong? Has something happened to Donna?" he asked as his double-breasted suit suddenly became unbearably tight.

"Oh, Robert," she replied almost in hysteria. "I think she tried to kill herself."

"What! What do you mean she tried to kill herself?"

"Her screaming woke me, so I went to see what was wrong. She had a wire wrapped around her neck; I think she was trying to strangle herself."

"What kind of wire?"

"It looked like a musical string."

"Oh shit, where are you?"

"St. Mary's Hospital, in San Francisco."

"Is she all right?"

"They had to give her a sedative, she's sleeping but I think they want to keep her a few days. Robert, she's scared to death, but there's something else…"

"Else, what else?"

"We found our Siamese cat in her bedroom, its neck was broken."

"Connie, she didn't try to kill herself and for God's sake she didn't kill your cat either. You know her better than that. A lot of things have been happening; I'll explain when I see you."

"If we're not home, we'll be at the hospital."

Robert turned to Carol, "Get me the next flight to San Francisco, and have Richard find someone to fill in for a few days."

Robert returned to his office, "I'm sorry, Dr. Morgan, but something has come up and I must leave."

"Nothing serious I hope."

"Just a personal problem."

"If there's anything I can do?" he offered, cocking his head to one side.

"No, no, thank you but I must be going."

Robert hit the buzzer, "What time does my flight leave?"

"Six-fifteen, and it's with American Airlines. I've ordered a one way ticket and it will be waiting for you at the ticket counter."

"Get Lieutenant Norris for me."

Robert began gathering his papers and clearing his desk.

"Buzzz."

"Joe?" he asked.

"Bob, what's up?"

"I have to go to San Francisco, I think our killer broke into Donna's bedroom and wrapped a harp string around her neck while she was sleeping. She's at St. Mary's Hospital in San Francisco, her sister thinks she killed their cat and may have tried to commit suicide," he babbled nervously. "I'll call when I find out what's going on."

"Where's the harp string?"

"I don't know."

"Find out, and let me know who's handling the case."

"Will do."

"What time is your flight?"

"Six-fifteen."

"I'll have an officer stop by and give you a lift to the airport; he'll be there by four-thirty."

Robert put his coat on and picked up his briefcase, "Make sure everything is locked before you leave."

"Carol nodded, "Everything will be taken care of, please be careful!"

Robert hurried to his car, when he had cleared the gate; he put the pedal to the metal.

Robert was packed and waiting when the unmarked police car pulled into his driveway, he walked onto the front porch and activated the security system.

"You can put your suitcase in here," he heard a familiar voice say.

Robert turned and saw Joe standing at the rear of the car with the trunk open.

"I wasn't expecting you," he said, a smile of appreciation flashing across his face.

"I was able to rearrange my schedule."

Fall was in full bloom and the huge maple trees that lined the quiet residential street were starting to show bare branches in readiness for the onslaught of winter. The vacuum created by their car sucked up the leaves on the roadway and blew them high into the air creating a multicolor whirlwind effect as they slowly drifted downward. But inside the car a strange quietness hovered like bad air.

"How is it our boy is able to do things even superman is unable to do?" Joe asked.

Robert shook his head, "When Donna and I checked into our cottage, there was champagne and flowers waiting for us. Richard and Shirley were the only ones who knew where we were going, but even they didn't know what room we would be in. How could he have known?"

"He's getting his information somewhere, maybe we should check your house and make sure it hasn't been bugged," Joe offered.

"I'd appreciate that. For some reason he has a personal vendetta against me, I've searched my archives to see if I had a patient who might want to do these things, but I can't find anything."

"Without getting into Doctor/Patient privileges, did Angel's description fit any of your patients?"

"Most of my patients are good hard working people," he said shaking his head. "I've had some tough looking hombres but none with the problems associated with this psychopath."

Joe took the LAX off ramp and followed the row of buildings until he saw the American Airlines sign, where he pulled to the curb.

"Thanks for the lift; I'll call you when I find out what's happening."

Joe nodded. "Do that, and good luck, partner."

Robert couldn't stop thinking of his wife and the terror she must have endured as he hurried toward the entrance. The terminal was busy and people were scurrying in every direction as if late for their plane, while others were lounging about with a bored look on their face.

He took his place at the end of a long line that ended at the ticket counter; the minutes seemed to drag until finally he was the next to be helped.

"I'm Doctor Robert Forrest and I've purchased a one way ticket to San Francisco."

The man typed Robert's name into the computer, "Can I see your identification, please?"

Robert handed him his driver's license. The man scrutinized Robert's identification, and then gave him his ticket, "Put this tag on your luggage and put it in the luggage bin; you'll be boarding at Door H. Thank you for flying American Airlines," he said sounding more like a robot that had been programmed than a human being. Robert picked up his suitcase and stepped aside. He did as was required and slid his suitcase in the baggage bin. Then he was off to his designated door where he was greeted by yet another long line.

Robert was deep in concentration when a female's voice boomed over the intercom, "Please fasten your safety belts, we will be landing at the San Francisco Airport in five minutes. We hope you've had a pleasant trip, and thank you for flying American Lines."

Robert fastened his safety belt and closed his eyes for a quick prayer. "Lord I don't know what I'd do if anything should happen to my wife, please give me the strength and insight to deal with all of this…Amen."

His fingers dug into the armrests as the tires touched the pavement, and then the airplane turned and taxied toward the terminal. In a matter of minutes the plane was readied for passengers to disembark.

Once off the plane, Robert followed the crowd to the baggage area where he claimed his suitcase. Outside the terminal, several taxicabs were waiting patiently, Robert approached to the first in line.

"Yes sir, I'm Regis, where would you like to go?" asked an elderly Black gentleman as he opened the trunk.

"Do you know where St. Mary's Hospital is?"

"Like the back of my hand," he said with a big grin.

"That's where I want to go," Robert said handing him his suitcase.

"I sure hope it's not serious," he stated as he placed the suitcase in the trunk.

"You look like you want to get to St. Mary's as fast as you can," he said looking in the rear view mirror.

"It's my wife."

"My wife died a couple of years ago, she'd been sick a long time, but no matter you're never ready. Just sit back and hold on, I know a short cut."

In no time, Regis was stopping in front of the Admittance Building. "That'll be thirty two-fifty."

Robert pulled out two twenty-dollar bills and handed them to Regis, "Keep the change."

"There's an information booth to your left, good luck, son."

Robert hurried to the booth, "Can I help you?" asked the middle-aged woman.

"My wife was admitted yesterday, her name is Donna Forrest."

"Donna Forrest," the woman repeated as she slowly typed her name into the computer. "She's in the psychiatric ward for further observation; you'll have to talk to her doctor if you want any further information."

"Who is her doctor and how do I get to the psychiatric ward?" Robert asked.

"Doctor Benjamin, go to the fifth floor and take a right."

Robert could hardly contain himself as he waited for the elevator door to open; and when it did, the ride was so smooth it was irritating to the point that he wasn't certain whether it was in fact moving at all. A few moments later, the door opened and he could see the nurse's station down the hallway; inside, two nurses were busily checking various files and making entries. When he approached the counter, the older of the two turned to face him, "Can I help you," she asked.

"I'm Dr. Robert Forrest, my wife Donna, was admitted yesterday."

"Can I see your identification, Doctor Forrest?"

Robert retrieved his wallet and handed her his medical credentials.

After scrutinizing Robert's credentials, "Thank you, Doctor, I'm Nurse Wilcott and Dr. Benjamin is her treating physician."

"How is she, and can I see her?" he asked nervously.

"She was extremely upset when she was admitted and it was necessary to sedate her. Of course you can see her, but I think you should speak with Dr. Benjamin first. Would you like me to page him?"

"Yes, of course."

Nurse Wilcott dialed a number and then hung up, "He will be calling back shortly."

"Thank you."

"Would you like some coffee while you wait?" she asked just as the phone began ringing. "Ward Five, Nurse Wilcott…Donna Forrest's husband is here and would like a word with you. Yes, Doctor, I'll tell him."

"Doctor Benjamin is on the third floor and is on his way up."

Robert nodded.

"Would you like that coffee now?"

"Please, cream only."

"Here you go, you look tired, this should help," she said handing him his coffee.

"Thank you, I am."

"I know you must be concerned about your wife, but Doctor Benjamin is one of our finest doctors."

"I'm sure he is," Robert replied as he heard footsteps from behind. He turned and saw a middle-aged man wearing dark trousers and a white medical jacket.

"Doctor Forrest, I presume?"

"Yes, and you must be Doctor Benjamin? How's my wife?" Robert asked nervously.

"You're wife is going through a very serious and traumatic experience. No one seems to know exactly what happened…or why. We do know she was in high spirits that evening, but come the next morning she was screaming and had a wire wrapped around her neck. Do you have any idea how or why this may have happened?"

Robert sat his coffee on the counter, "Yes, I do. Can we go somewhere and talk?

"Yes, of course," he answered, unsure of how to respond to Robert's unanticipated reaction.

Dr. Benjamin escorted Robert to his office, "Have a seat; I must admit, you do have my full attention."

"Thank you. First, I must tell you that I'm also a psychiatrist and that I'm involved in helping the Los Angeles Police find a serial killer."

"I thought you looked familiar, I believe I saw you on television."

"Since that interview, the killer has taken a personal vendetta against me and my wife and has been stalking us.

Robert proceeded to unfold the mysterious events that took place over the past several weeks.

"Well Doctor, if he's trying to scare you, he's certainly doing a fine job with Donna. Did you say that this Lieutenant Norris is aware of what's going on here in San Francisco?"

"Yes he is."

Dr. Benjamin shrugged his shoulders, "What do you want us to do, Doctor? We're a hospital, our nurses aren't policemen, and it seems as long as your wife remains here we're putting everyone's lives in jeopardy."

"What I would like," Robert said pausing for a moment to curb his mounting anxieties, "is to have Donna stay here until she's capable of traveling. At that time, I will have her transferred to whatever facility is best for her. In the meantime, I'll ask Lieutenant Norris to call the San Francisco Police Department and have a policeman guard her until she's well enough to be moved. I do realize her being here puts your staff at risk, that's why I thought it best you know why this has happened."

Dr. Benjamin took a deep breath, "I appreciate your honesty," and then he paused for the longest moment. Robert knew he had a monumental decision to make, and he could see by his expression that he was very concerned about the situation. "Okay," he finally replied. "If you can arrange to have a policeman guard her, I'll see that she stays here until she can be moved. That's the best I can do."

"Thank you. If I can use your phone, I'd like to call Lieutenant Norris?"

"Certainly," he said pointing to the phone on his desk.

"When I'm through, I'd like to see my wife?"

"Turn to your left as you leave my office, your wife is in room Five-thirty-two. We'll do all we can to help," he promised.

"Thank you," Robert said, feeling as if a great burden had just been lifted from his shoulders.

"Joe, this is Bob, I'm at St. Mary's Hospital. I've just spoken with Doctor Benjamin and he says if we can arrange a police guard, Donna can stay here until she recovers enough to be moved."

"Good; would you like me to call San Francisco PD?"

"Oh brother would I," Robert said, relieved that Joe volunteered.

"No problem, I'll ask that they send a plainclothes officer so it won't look so conspicuous. How's Donna?"

"I haven't seen her yet, I wanted to talk to you first."

"Hang in there; everything's going to be fine."

Robert read the number on every door until he came to Donna's room. He pushed the heavy door open; his heart sank when he saw his wife lying in bed. She looked so helpless. He tiptoed over and gave her a tender kiss on her forehead, praying that she would respond with the smile he loved so much. But instead, she lay as if in a comma, her face without expression and no smile on her lips.

Robert held her hand, hoping the love in his heart might somehow awaken her like he had seen in so many movies. But this was not the silver screen.

"How could I have let this happen?" he asked as he gently stroked her hair. Robert was so angry with himself for breaking his promise to Donna, and hurt because she was the one to pay for his involvement. Guilt soared, and he could not bring himself to leave her side as he continued to pray for her slightest movement. Several times he took her pulse just to reassure himself that she was still alive.

Finally in the wee hours of the morning and out of complete exhaustion, Robert finally succumbed to the need for sleep. "Doctor Forrest," a voice came booming from a far and distant zone. Robert opened his weary eyes; slowly the blurred vision transformed into the likeness of Dr. Morgan. Morgan was standing over him with his hand was inside his mouth and grasping onto his tongue. In a sinister tone, Morgan began speaking, "I think it's best we remove this." The words sent shivers to the depths of his soul and his body began shaking and quivering as if in a violent convulsion. Quickly, he grabbed onto Morgan's hand in an attempt to keep it from ripping his tongue from his mouth. "Doctor Forrest," the voice boomed again, only louder. Again his body trembled violently as he continued to hold a grip lock on Morgan's hand. Suddenly the hand began to release its hold on his tongue and it slipped from his mouth. "Ahhhggg...ahhhggg," he screamed as his body continued shaking uncontrollably.

"Doctor Forrest, wake up." But this time it was a female's voice. His eyes finally began to focus and this time it was not Morgan standing over him, but Nurse Walcott, and she was massaging her hand. "Are you, okay?" she asked apprehensively.

Robert nodded, quickly reaching into his mouth and franticly searching for his tongue.

"There's a policeman to see you," she said with a troubled look on her face.

"I'm sorry," he said nervously, his face showing his embarrassment.

"Are you sure you're, okay," she asked again.

Robert stood up and began straightening his clothing, "It was just a bad dream. Please, send him in."

Nurse Wilcott departed and shortly thereafter a plain-clothes officer entered.

"I'm Doctor Forrest," he said shaking his hand.

"Nice to meet you, Doctor, I'm Detective Burns."

"Did anyone explain why you're here?"

"Lieutenant Norris from LAPD explained everything. He said the guy's pretty clever and that I best be on my toes, but I assure you I will guard her with my life!"

"Thank you, Detective Burns, I feel better all ready."

At that moment the door opened and Connie and Jim walked in.

"Oh Robert, I'm so sorry," she said giving him a hug.

Robert nodded, barely able to contain his emotions.

"Jim thanks for coming."

"Robert, you look so tired, why don't you and Jim go home so you can get some sleep. I'll stay with Donna."

"Come on Robert, you need to get some shuteye," Jim urged.

Robert nodded. "Call me if she comes to."

Connie shook her head, "I will, now go get some rest."

Chapter Ten

Good evening, Detective Burns," Robert greeted, smiling for the first time in days.

"Good evening, I take it Doctor Benjamin told you Donna was awake?"

"He did, and I can't tell you how much you and your fellow officers guarding her have meant."

Robert opened the door, Donna and Nurse Wilcott were conversing, his heart melted when he saw the joy on her face when their eyes met. He stood unable to move, smiling from ear to ear as a large knot formed in his throat. Suddenly all the pain and anguish was gone and the feeling of overwhelming joy filled his heart. Donna held out her arms and Robert rushed to her side. "Oh Baby, I'm so sorry," he said embracing her.

"Robert, I'm so scared," she said her voice quivering uncontrollably. "Please, hold me."

"It's okay; everything's going to be all right. I've got you and no one's going to hurt you anymore, I promise."

"Just hold me; I need you to hold me."

He could feel her body trembling and hear her sobbing as she lay her head on his shoulder; he pulled a tissue from its container and handed it to her.

Donna wiped the tears from her eyes, "I know I need to control myself, but I can't. I feel like I can't breath."

"Shhh," he said.

"Excuse me, Doctor Forrest," Nurse Wilcott apologized. "I was about to give Donna her medication, but if you like, it can wait until you've had time to talk."

"I think its best she takes it now, but I'd like to stay until she falls asleep."

Without answering Nurse Wilcott turned to Donna and handed her two paper cups, one containing her medication and the other water to drink, "This will help you relax."

Donna forced a smiled and did as she was told.

"That's a good, girl," Nurse Wilcott praised. Then she turned to Robert, "She'll fall asleep soon, and you can stay as long as you like." Nurse Wilcott turned back to Donna, "You don't have to worry, your cute husband will be right here and those big policemen outside are here to protect you, too."

Robert watched as the pills began to do their magic. Donna's eyes began to grow heavy and her breathing began to slow, and then a calm peaceful serene look replaced her tense expression. The long hours were taking their toll and Robert found himself nodding off now and then only to be awakened by Nurse Wilcott taking Donna's vital signs. "Go back to sleep," she would say, "I'll wake you if there's any change."

He felt the gentle tug on his shoulder, and his hand shot toward his mouth to feel his tongue He raised his head as his dazed mind fought to go from a subliminal state to a conscious one. Finally the blurring figure came into focus. "Connie?" he asked.

"Why don't you go home, I'll call if there's any change."

Robert nodded, knowing he was completely exhausted.

"Good morning, Doctor Forrest," said the plain-clothes officer as Robert exited the room.

"Detective Talley?" Robert asked, stunned and glancing at his watch, "I was expecting to see Detective Burns, I didn't realize it was so late."

"Yeah, Dave went home hours ago."

"That sounds like a good idea," he said rubbing the back of his neck. "I'll see you later."

"Good night, Doctor," Talley replied as he reopened the book he was reading.

Talley was still immersed in his book when the door opened and this time Connie stepped outside, "Its two-thirty, will you call me if there's any change."

Talley nodded, and then warned her of the bars just closing and the possibility of drinking drivers on the streets. He watched until Connie disappeared down the hallway before walking to the water cooler and taking a drink of cold water in an attempt to fight the urge to sleep. Returning to his chair, he once again submersed himself in the novel. He was brought back to reality when he heard footsteps rapidly heading his direction.

"It's only me," the man said as he approached. Talley didn't recognize him, but he was wearing a San Francisco PD uniform. "The Lieutenant thought you might want something to eat," he said handing Talley a MacDonald's bag.

"Hey, that sounds great!" he said opening the bag and looking inside. "Would you mind watching the door while I take a leak and wash my hands?"

"No problem," the officer replied casually as if not being in any hurry to leave.

"Thanks, I won't be long."

"Take your time," he said sitting in Talley's chair and picking up the book he had been reading, "Hollywood...Vice or Versa by Joe Noonkester," he read out loud. "Good book."

"Yeah, it helps make the night go faster."

The officer watched Talley's every step until he was out of sight, then his eyes turned toward the door. He slowly made his way to Donna's side. "So they think they can keep me from you, do they? I go where I want and when I want!" He studied Donna's beautiful but vulnerable face. "But my patience is running thin!" He reached down and pulled Donna's hospital issued nightgown aside, exposing her left breast. A smile of power crossed his lips as he leaned over and whispered in her ear, "Very nice my little Angel, soon I will enjoy all you have to offer."

He began chuckling as he removed Donna's wedding ring from her finger. "We've done this before, haven't we? I'd give someone's right hand to see the look on your cheating husband's face when he sees this gone again. I'll be in touch."

Talley exited the restroom, still drying his hands and face with a paper towel as he walked toward his post. His heart nearly stopped when the uniformed officer was no where to be seen. Instantly, he knew he had been had.

He unleashed his revolver and began running down the hallway. He stopped outside Donna's room and placed his ear on the door, listening for any sounds. All was silent. He slowly pushed the door open, keeping his body safely behind the wall. He reached inside and switched the light on. Donna was in bed and her left breast was exposed, but he couldn't tell whether she was breathing or not.

He scanned the room, it was empty. He stowed his gun and quickly covered Donnas' breast. He placed his finger on her neck and breathed a sigh of relief when he found a strong healthy pulse. "Oh God, thank you," he praised.

Talley quickly summoned a nurse, and then walked out into the hallway.

In no time a nurse was scurrying toward his location. "Stay with her," Talley ordered. "Where's the nearest phone?"

"In the nurse's station, dial nine to get an outside number. What's wrong?"

Without answering, Talley hastened to the Nurse's station and dialed nine-nine-eleven.

"Police department," the voice stated.

"I'm Detective Talley and I'm at St. Mary's Hospital, we have a man impersonating a police officer. He's a male Caucasian in his fifties, six feet, two hundred pounds, brown hair and mustache, and he's wearing a San Francisco PD uniform. He was last seen on the fifth floor, approximately five minutes ago but he may have a vehicle nearby. Use caution, he has a gun and is wanted for at least six serial killings in the Los Angeles area."

"That's a roger, Detective Talley. I'll put out a broadcast."

Talley took a deep breath and shook his head in disgust for being fooled so easily, and yet feeling so fortunate that the killer hadn't taken greater advantage of his moment of apathy and stupidity.

He removed his Lieutenant's home phone number from his wallet, "Yeah," the man answered in a gruff voice, "Who's this?"

"Lieutenant, this is Detective Talley at St. Mary's Hospital, we have a problem..."

Robert could see Talley and two uniformed officers conversing as he and Connie hurried in their location.

"I got here as quickly as I could, what's wrong?" Robert asked almost frantically.

"Your wife is fine, but we did have a visitor," Talley replied.

"A visitor, what do you mean? What happened?"

"About four AM..." and Talley related the incidence exactly as it occurred.

Robert was floored; he could not believe what he was hearing.

"Excuse me, but I have to see how my wife is," he said disgustedly.

Donna was sedated and still sleeping comfortably. He sat next to her and took her hand in his and kissed it delicately. It came without warning, like a sucker punch in the stomach, causing his heart to momentarily halt. He gasped trying to catch his breath. "Oh, nooo..." he moaned as his face turned white as a ghost.

"She's okay, Robert, she's under medication," Connie said trying to calm him down.

"No, no," he said shaking his head and holding Donna's hand up so Connie could see her naked finger. "He's done it again; he's taken her wedding ring."

Connie stated smugly, "The hospital probably has it, its hospital policy that they remove all jewelry."

"Not this time, I asked under the circumstances that they not take it."

Connie shrugged, not knowing what to say.

"Wait here, I've got to get her somewhere she'll be safe. She may never recover if she finds that her ring is missing again."

"What are you going to do?"

"I'm going to call the Meadows Sanitarium in Los Angeles and make arrangements for her to stay there. It's a place she'll be safe until she's well enough to come home."

Connie sat down in Robert's chair and picked up her little sister's hand.

Robert quickly exited the room. "Talley," Robert stated sternly, "I'm going to make a phone call and other than her sister, I don't want anyone in her room while I'm gone."

"Yes sir!" he replied, his face still flushed with embarrassment.

Robert made a bee-line for the nurse's station without further discussion.

"I'm sorry, Doctor Forrest," the nurse on duty apologized. "I had no idea what was going on."

"Can I use your phone, please?"

The nurse nodded.

"Operator," a female voice said.

"I'd like the number for the Meadows Sanitarium in Los Angeles," he asked as he removed a pen and note pad from his pocket.

"One moment please," the operator replied, and then a recording said, "The number is…"

Robert returned to Donna's room. "Connie," he said softly.

"I've made arrangements for Donna to be transferred. They'll be sending an unmarked ambulance so no one will know who's in it or where it's going. I think it best Donna not know her ring has been stolen at this time."

Connie nodded in agreement.

"I'll go with her in the ambulance, why don't you go home and get some sleep," he said kissing her on her forehead.

Connie nodded, "Okay, but let me know what's going on."

"I will, sis…and thanks for your help," he said fighting back his emotions.

Connie started to leave but stopped and threw her arms around Robert's neck. "Take care of my little sister," she whispered.

"I will, I promise," Robert said trying to smile but inside his body was trembling and his mind numb from all the stress.

"Where are we going?" Donna asked groggily as she momentarily regained semi-consciousness. "Robert, where's Con…?" she murmured as her eyes rolled back into her head and her eyelids closed and she drifted back into unconsciousness.

"We're going where you'll be safe," Robert whispered, knowing that she was unable to hear him.

The paramedic inflated the cup and began taking Donna's blood pressure. "Her blood pressure is normal for the medication she's under," he said trying to reassure Robert that she was in good hands. "Tell me," he said looking somewhat puzzled. "Isn't it kind of unusual for us to be taking a patient all the way from San Francisco to Beverly Hills, are you some kind of VIP or is she…"

"She's my wife, damn it, and that's all you need to know," Robert snorted.

"Hey, I didn't mean anything. I was just curious that's all, don't be so uptight."

Robert ran his fingers through his hair, "I'm sorry, it's been a long day. And No I'm not a VIP; however, Doctor Shilling is a good friend."

"And the reason for the unmarked ambulance?" the paramedic asked.

"The unmarked ambulance?" Robert repeated. "Nooo…particular reason," he shrugged. "I guess a little less expensive," he stated caught off guard by the medics prying and him failing miserably when having to come up with an off-the-cuff explanation.

"Well Doctor, we all have to cut corners, don't we? She'll never know anyway, she'll be sleeping the whole trip," he said amusingly.

Robert held Donna's hand, as mile after mile and hour after hour passed. Throughout the trip, he found himself nodding off only to be awakened by the noise of a large freight truck passing. Finally the night began to give way to the awakening of a new dawn, and Robert watched in awe as the rising sun burst onto the horizon like a giant fireball sent down from the heavens.

Leaving Interstate Five and its light traffic, they turned onto the San Diego Freeway south bound to mingle with its multitudes of cars seemingly racing one another for that elusive opening in traffic. Then the inevitable red lights began appearing as the road racers hit their brakes and their cars slowed to a crawl and they were forced to inch their way toward their destination.

They took the Sunset Blvd off-ramp toward Beverly Hills, then onto Duff Place, a windy narrow road that was carved into the heavily wooded hillsides, their autumn leaves turning into a frenzy of gold's and yellow's.

They worked their way up the hillside until they came to a long stoned wall with a small paved road running parallel to it. They followed the paved road until they came to a guardhouse with a large wrought iron-gate. The driver stopped in front of the gate and the security guard walked over to the ambulance.

"Hey, Terry," the driver said handing the guard his Patients Form, listing Donna Forrest as the patient and authorized by Dr. Shilling.

"Hi, Mel, is anyone inside other than Tom and Mrs. Forrest?"

"Mrs. Forrest's husband is with her."

"Hang on," Terry ordered and he walked to the rear of the ambulance and opened the door.

"I need to see your ID, sir," he requested.

Robert complied, happy to observe such tight security.

The guard went inside the guardhouse and copied the information from Robert's ID. He returned to the ambulance and gave Robert his visitor's pass, "Be sure to wear this at all time and don't go anywhere you are not authorized to go," he warned.

"Okay Mel, I'll call and let them know you're coming.

"This is really a beautiful place," Robert said looking around the manicured grounds.

"Have you been here before?" Tom asked.

"Yes, but it's been quite a while. I see they're still very careful of who comes and goes."

"That's for sure, they have the finest security system I've ever seen, and there's only one way in and one way out."

The ten-acre Meadows mansion looked more like a southern plantation than a hospital. Mel pulled into the admittance area and parked between two other ambulances. As soon as he had stopped, two rather muscular medical attendants approached.

"Hi guys," Mel said handing them his paperwork.

One attendant opened the ambulance door and confronted Robert, "Doctor Forrest, Doctor Shilling would like to see you in his office. I've been told you know where it is."

"Yes, I do."

"We'll take Donna to her room while you see Doctor Shilling. He'll show you to your wife's room."

"Thank you," Robert replied.

"Can I help you?" another muscular male attendant asked as Robert entered the building.

"I'm Doctor Forrest; I'm supposed to meet with Doctor Shilling in his office."

The attendant wrote down Robert's guest pass number, "His office is the second door on the left."

Robert approached Dr. Schilling's office and knocked on the door.

"Robert, it's good to see you, please come in," he said.

"It's been a long time," Robert remarked, shaking his hand. "I wish it were under better circumstances."

"Me too," Dr. Shilling said looking over the brim of his reading glasses. "I've been very concerned since you told me what has happened. I don't want to sound pompous but our security system is unequaled."

Robert smiled. "I'm very impressed with your staff."

"As you know, we have some very high profile patients and their safety and privacy is a must. But our safety goes much deeper than what you've seen, the fifteen-foot high fence you saw completely surrounds our ten-acre grounds and security cameras are strategically located on top. These cameras are monitored twenty-four hour's a day and no one gets through the front gate without prior authorization from me and only me."

"That's why I thought it best to have Donna brought here, this guy's so clever and he seems to penetrate even the best of security systems."

"Robert, we've been friends for how many years now…twenty, twenty-two? Let me tell you, Donna will be safe here, I guarantee it."

"Thanks Charles, I do feel better. Lieutenant Norris is giving me a lift home; can I see Donna before he gets here?"

"We can go right now, but first let me call the front gate so they will be expecting him."

Dr. Shilling hit the front gate speed dial, "Terry, a Lieutenant Joe Norris from the LAPD will be picking up Doctor Forrest. Let him in, and they have my authorization to leave the grounds."

"Yes sir, I've logged in your authorization. Thank you, sir."

"Now let's go see how your lovely wife is doing."

They took the elevator to the third floor, and when the door opened they were only a few yards from the nurse's station, inside was a registered nurse and two muscular male attendants.

"Robert, this is Nurse Braddock and Jim and Ted. Robert is a dear friend of mine, so I want you to do all you can to make his wife as comfortable as possible."

Chapter Eleven

It was ten PM and everyone had filtered out of the Special Task Force office until only Joe remained, all lighting was off except for the small lamp sitting on his desk. The coroner's reports were lying in front of Joe and he was systematically examining each one.

All five victims had been killed in the same vicious manner and each other than Victim-Five, had been cleansed of all blood and wiped down with alcohol before being dropped off. Victim-Five, however, was found inside his shower and there was no attempt to cleanse his body. But what puzzled Joe the most, was the complete opposite description of the suspect by two separate eyewitnesses. The first, even though it was only a partial, was quite certain of what he saw. His description was that of a male Caucasian in his fifties, approximately six feet tall, short dark brown hair, very neat in appearance and driving a new or near new dark green or black vehicle. The other witness watched as the suspect killed two of his best friends, Victims Four and Five. His description was that of a male Caucasian in his sixties, wrinkled face with long stringy brown hair and a scraggily beard, wearing old clothes and very dirty in appearance. One suspect appears to be quite wealthy while the other is apparently living in poverty. What could these two opposites possibly have in common? And how could there be two totally different descriptions when the coroner's in-depth study revealed that the same person committed all the murders? But could there actually be two suspects? And could they be working together?"

Joe was deep in concentration when all of a sudden the bright overhead lights flashed on. "Don't you think it's about time you go home," a voice barked from behind.

"Captain, I didn't hear you come in. You're working kind of late too, aren't you?" Joe asked leaning back in his chair.

"It seems as though we all are," he chuckled. "Come into my office I have something to give you."

"We've finally gotten a break," he said handing Joe an envelope.

Joe opened the envelope and pulled out the document.

"A search warrant?" he asked with a confused look on his face. "What's going on, Captain?"

"Yes, a search warrant, and that's the name and address of our serial killer. I knew you'd be pleased," he smiled proudly.

"But…"

"I know, I know. I should have let you know," he interrupted. "But I just received the information while I was attending a social function and I wanted to give it to you personally…to see the look on your face. Judge Miley was there and happily signed it."

"That's great, Captain," Joe responded with a big smile.

"Yes, it is. I want a stakeout of the suspect's apartment ASAP, and I don't want anyone approaching until we're sure our boy's inside. I want an arrest!" the Captain ordered.

"If he's there, we'll get him," Joe assured him. "I'll have Slater and Williams take the first shift."

"Be sure and keep me informed," Murdock said.

Joe nodded, "Do you feel all right, your voice sounds a little different?"

"I feel fine; I just haven't been getting the sleep that I require."

"I understand, Captain, it's been a drain on all of us."

"And while we're on the subject, I think it's time you to call it a night. I'll only be a minute and when I walk out," he chuckled, "I don't want to see that ugly mug of yours and that's an order."

"You're right of course; Colleen has almost forgotten what I look like. But I do have one question."

. "It can wait until morning…Good-night, Joe."

"Would you like some coffee," Slater asked as he retrieved the thermos from the back seat.

Williams nodded, "Man, it's getting cold," he said breathing onto his hands and rubbing them together.

Slater removed two Styrofoam cups from a paper bag and filled them with hot coffee and handed one to Williams.

"I just don't like working these hours, nights are for sleeping, and especially on such short notice," Williams complained.

Slater glanced at his watch, four-thirty AM. "At least the worst is over, only three and a half hours to go," he said trying to speak and yawn at the same time.

"Don't do that," Williams grumbled, starting a long slow yawn himself.

Joe rolled over and turned the alarm clock off.

"I'll make some coffee while you take your shower," Colleen said giving Joe a quick kiss.

"Thanks babe," he said trying to muster the energy to get out of bed. "I'm not sure this old body's going to last much longer," he said rubbing the small of his back.

"Don't talk like that you big ole' teddy bear," she chuckled. "Go take your shower while I fix breakfast."

"Okay, pilgrim," Joe chuckled as he strolled toward the bathroom doing his famous John Wayne walk.

"You big ham," she chuckled. "Why do all you men want to be John Wayne?"

"There he is," Williams said pointing to the suspect's apartment.

Slater picked up the mic, "Six-W-Ten, this is Six-W-One, come in.

"Go ahead Slater; what's happening?"

"Joe, our suspect has just entered his apartment."

"Are you sure it's him."

"It's him, he looks just like Angel described."

"Good. When Sgt. Slater gives the word, I want Six-Adam-thirty-three to station themselves at the rear of the apartment. There's no back door but there is a bathroom window on the east side. Make sure he doesn't climb out. Remember, he's wanted for murder and I want everyone to take the necessary precautions, but I don't want him to escape either."

"Hear that, guys, let's be careful. Six-Adam-thirty-three...go," Slater ordered.

Slater gave Six-Adam-thirty-three time to get into position, and then accompanied by Six-Adam-seventy-five, he and Williams approached the front door with weapons drawn.

Slater pounded on the front door, "Police, we have a search warrant, open the door."

When there was no immediate response, he kicked the door and it flew open crashing into the wall behind. Slowly and cautiously, he entered the front room, his eyes scanning every object and his finger on the trigger and ready to respond to any dangers he might confront.

The front room was empty. Slater quickly moved to the kitchen and then the bathroom, they were also empty. That left only the bedroom. Without saying a word, he motioned for one of the uniformed officers to remain and guard the front door. Williams positioned himself on one side of the bedroom door while Slater stationed himself on the other. Slater slowly turned the doorknob and pushed door open, and then listened for any sounds or possible movements. When no sounds were heard, he peered around the door jam. "The bedroom looks empty," he conveyed.

The room contained only a queen-size bed and two wooden double bi-folding doors that was obviously the closet. With officers on each side of the bi-folding doors and Slater in a position to see directly inside the closet when the doors opened, Slater shouted, "Police, come out with your hands up,"

There was no response.

"We know you're in the closet, come out with your hands up," he ordered again.

The silence was deafening.

Slater squeezed his trigger in anticipation of the imminent confrontation, the hammer rising like a deadly cobra about to strike its prey. Then he motioned for both bi-folding doors to be opened."

Clothes filled the closet, but there were no signs of the suspect.

"What the Hell's going on?" He asked looking around the room with a bewildered look on his face. "Is he some kind of magician or what?" Slater paused for a moment, "We know he's smart, but he can't disappear into thin air."

He walked back into the front room, stopped and began sniffing. "What's that strange scent?"

Williams began sniffing, "It smells like rubber, or sulfur, or some kind of chemical."

Slater approached the kitchen cabinet where the smell might be coming from. He opened the door but the cabinet was empty

"Yes sir, they're inside," Slater heard the officer guarding the front door saying.

Slater turned to face Joe as he entered the apartment, "I got here as fast as I could, did you get him?"

Slater shook his head.

"What happened?"

"He just vanished…poof," Slater said holding his hands in mid-air. "We waited until he got inside and then surrounded the apartment, he didn't leave but I don't know where he went either."

Joe began sniffing the air, "What's that smell?"

"I don't know, we smelled it too but we haven't determined where it's coming from."

"Williams, go call latent prints," Joe ordered.

After Williams had left, "What do you think, Joe?" Slater asked.

"We know he's clever, so go over everything with a fine toothed comb," he said in an irritated tone.

Joe looked around the room. "You're sure he came in?"

"Yeah, we all saw him."

"Well he didn't just vanish, have you looked for a concealed door or anything like that?"

"Not yet, we haven't had time."

Joe called to the officer guarding the front door, "Gary, don't let anyone in until Sergeant Slater says its okay."

"Yes, Lieutenant," he replied.

Ted," he said to the other officer, "tell the officers outside to continue securing the premises and to stop anyone they might find. Tell them to stay where they are until Sergeant Slater personally dismisses them."

Joe and Slater then combed every inch in the apartment, but to no avail.

Joe shrugged, "I guess I better go tell Murdock the good news. Don't worry, it's not your fault," Joe said slapping Slater on his shoulder. "Let me know if you do come up with anything."

"Will do," Slater said breathing a little easier. "Thanks, Joe."

Joe nodded, "See you at the office."

Joe pulled into the parking lot and took a deep breath when he saw Murdock's car. "You're not going to be very happy," he said as he turned to take the long dreaded walk to Captain's office.

"Good morning, Lieutenant," the desk officer remarked as Joe passed.

"Good morning," Joe replied, trying to sound as cheerful as he could under the circumstances.

He climbed the stairs leading to the Special Task Force office, "Good morning, Lieutenant," Detective Sharon Wilson greeted. "Captain Murdock wants to see you the minute you arrive."

Joe nodded, "I might as well get this over," he said under his breath.

Joe felt like a lamb going to slaughter as he approached Murdock's office, he paused for a moment taking a deep breath and then knocked soundly on the door.

"Come in," he heard Murdock's gruff voice say.

Murdock was sitting at his desk going over paperwork.

"Good morning, Captain. I just came from Lexington and I wish I had better news," he said, his embarrassment showing. "Slater and

126

Williams are still at the apartment and Latent Prints are on their way."

"What are you talking about?"

"The search warrant, you wanted me to let you know what happened."

"Search warrant?" Murdock asked, his face drawing a blank.

"Yes Captain, the search warrant you gave me last night."

"I gave you a search warrant last night?"

"Yes, the one signed by Judge Miley."

"What are you talking about, are you out of your mind? I did nothing of the sort, and I certainly wasn't here last night," he said, his coarse voice almost shouting.

"Now just a minute," Joe shot back. "Are you saying you weren't here last night?"

"Of course I wasn't here last night. I went home early yesterday, you know that," he said trying to calm himself and Joe down. "Joe, you've been working too hard, I think you need to take a day off."

"Well I'll let you in on a little secret, Captain, someone was here last night and he sat right there at your desk and I talked with him for over fifteen minutes. And if it wasn't you, then you have a twin brother."

Murdock shook his head, and then without saying a word he walked over to the window and stood gazing out onto the parking lot below.

Joe was embroiled, he was not hallucinating and he wasn't going to be intimidated by anyone, even Murdock who was like a father to him. Joe finally broke the silence; "Well then, what did you want to see me about?"

Murdock turned to face Joe, "I've received a memorandum from SID about some high tech equipment you've signed out. If you're still using them, you'll need to send a memorandum; you know you can only check them out for thirty days."

"I did what? Can I see the memorandum?"

Murdock handed it to him and Joe began reading.

"This can't be right; I haven't checked out any equipment. I've known Rick Hansen for years; I'll call him and clear this up."

Joe dialed Property Division and pushed the intercom button so Murdock could listen.

"SID, Sergeant Hansen."

"Rick, this is Joe Norris, I've just received a memorandum stating that I checked out some hi tech equipment."

"Yes Joe, I'm sorry but I have to send a memorandum on any equipment that's past due. Just send me a memorandum saying you're still using the equipment and I can give you another thirty days."

"Rick, it says that you personally released the equipment to me."

"I sure did, remember I even had Brad Chapman help carry the equipment to your car. Is something wrong?"

"Rick, are you sure it was me?"

"Am I sure it was you? Joe, how many years have we known each other, of course I'm sure it was you. Is there some kind of problem?"

"No, I'll get a memorandum back to you as soon as I can."

Joe shook his head, "Something very strange is going on. First, someone who looks just like you gives me a search warrant. We stake out the suspect's apartment and follow him inside, but he's gone…vanished! Then someone who looks exactly like me goes to SID and checks out…" and Joe begins reading the list of equipment, "(six) Hi tech surveillance kits including television monitors, recording and dubbing machines with cables and attachments, (twenty-four) Phone bugging devices, (twenty-four) Room recording audio and video devices, (twenty-four) Electric tracking devices with monitors, (twelve) Navy seal military night cat binoculars, (twelve) Hearing aid devices, (twenty-four) Remote ink pen's with audio and video reception…and signs my name. What's going on?" Then Joe slowly begins looking around the room.

Murdock picks up on Joe's drift. "You know, I had the strangest feeling when I sat down at my desk this morning…small things were not where I had left them."

"That's how he's doing it," Joe said as if a light bulb had been switched to the On position.

"Doing what?" Murdock asked.

"Don't you see? He knows everything; every thing we say and everything we're about to do."

"You don't mean to imply that he's bugged my office?" Murdock asked as he began picking up and scrutinizing various items on his desk.

"What I'm saying, Captain, is far worse. He's bugged the whole Task Force.

Murdock raised his hand, "Shhh...did you hear that?"

There was a faint chuckling sound coming from somewhere.

"There it is again," Murdock snorted as he looked in the direction of the laughter.

It was coming from a pen set sitting on Murdock's desk.

"What the Hell?" Murdock gasped.

"You're finally catching on," the voice acknowledged. "You're so pathetic, how many clues do I have to give you before you," and he began chuckling again, "you and all of your fine minds discover what's really going on? If you can't do that, how do you ever expect to catch me?"

"Can you hear me?" Joe asked trying to restrain his anger.

"I hear you and I can see you, too!" he chuckled softly.

"For God's sake, for what sick purpose are you doing this?" Joe fumed.

"Now, now, hold your tongue or I will," he retorted coldly.

"Why are you doing this, and what are you trying to tell us?" Joe asked.

"Can't you figure anything out for yourself? You were on the right track when you asked about a secret door...but your little morons couldn't find it. I have to go now...and let you boys do what you do best?" he mocked sarcastically. "But I'll be seeing you, and very soon. Have a nice day."

"Joe, call SID and have them send someone, right now. I want this whole damn department combed. That bastard is making a mockery out me, you, and every other investigator working here. I won't have it," Murdock said slamming his fist on his desk as anger overtook him.

"Now, now, you boys do behave…next time I might not be in such a good mood," the voice scolded.

Murdock looked at Joe, and then said almost whispering, "I want this whole area cleared until it has been thoroughly checked."

"SID, Sergeant Talbert."

"Mike, this is Joe Norris."

"Hey Joe, what can I do for you?"

"Captain Murdock would like…" and Joe winced as he continued, "for you to send your best men to the Special Task Force office…we've been bugged."

"Bugged? The Special Task Force?" he asked not believing what he had just heard.

"He wants this kept QT and he wants them, now!"

"We'll be there in thirty minutes" Talbert promised.

Joe relayed the information to Murdock.

"I can handle this from here. I want you to personally conduct the search on Lexington. There must be something there that this…" and then Murdock paused looking down at the pen set on his desk, "that our boy wants us to find."

Joe stuck his head inside the room, "Carter, grab your coat and come with me."

As Joe and Carter neared the suspect's apartment, they could see crews from CBS and NBC television parked in front of the location and Slater standing by the front door talking to reporters.

Joe pulled to the curb and they were instantly bombarded by reporters with cameras rolling. "Lieutenant, does this mean that you now know the identity of the serial killer?" one reporter asked.

"I have no comment at this time," Joe replied.

"Lieutenant," another reporter stated, "we've received information that you now know the identity of the suspect?"

Joe turned to the reporter, "I'm sorry, but I cannot comment at this time."

"Come on, Lieutenant, didn't you ask us to meet you here because you wanted to make a statement?" remarked the first reporter.

Joe stopped when he heard the remark and turned to face the reporters, "I tell you what," Joe said pausing for a moment. "Give me a few minutes and when I return I will give you a statement."

"We are live at sixty-four-fourteen Lexington Avenue where police are at this very moment conducting a search of an apartment believed to belong to the suspect in the heinous murders of Barry Snider and five others. We'll be standing by for a live update with Lieutenant Joe Norris of the Special Task Force in just a few moments. This is Murray Fredericks...reporting live from Hollywood."

Joe motioned for Slater to follow him inside, "What's going on?"

"I don't know," Slater shrugged. "Latent Prints and the Photo Lab were here, when all of a sudden television crews started showing up. They said you wanted to make a statement."

"That bastard," Joe said angrily.

"What's going on?"

"We're being set up. It's a long story and it can wait until we're through here. What have you found?"

"Nothing," Slater replied.

"Have you looked for any secret doors or passages?"

"Yeah, but we couldn't find anything."

"Well let's take another look and make sure we're not overlooking anything?"

"You're the boss, but we went over everything with a fine toothed comb."

"Hi, Lieutenant," Randy greeted and then turning to Slater. "I've finished taking the photo's you wanted."

"Randy;" Joe interrupted, "would you mind waiting a few minutes before you leave?"

"Sure," Randy said shrugging his shoulders.

Joe approached a large built-in cabinet in the living room and began pushing and pulling on various knobs and handles. When his actions did not produce any results, his eyes turned to the area where the cabinet and the wall came together. He tried pulling the two apart but they would not budge. Then he began scrutinizing the floor for any signs of scratches that might indicate that the cabinet had been moved or swung out, but there was none. Then he stepped back for an over all view of the cabinet.

"What are you looking for?" Slater asked.

"A secret door," he said uncertain if there was actually a secret door hidden somewhere or if the suspect was merely making a fool of him.

"A secret door?"

"Well he went somewhere, didn't he?" Joe grumbled.

They searched every inch of the bathroom, but found nothing. Then they checked the bedroom and even moved the bed to examine the floor underneath, but again nothing. They checked the closet for every conceivable possibility, but still nothing.

The only place they hadn't searched was the kitchen. Joe began systematically scanning the area, but his eyes kept returning to the refrigerator. It couldn't be he thought, but the more he looked at the refrigerator the more sense it made. "That's it, it's such an obvious place no one would ever think of looking there," he said out loud. He grasped the refrigerator and pulled it away from the wall. Sure enough, on the wall behind the refrigerator was a small door. Joe reached in the apparent finger hole and pressed on the lock mechanism and pushed the door open. Just like the locks on my boat, he thought as he shined his flashlight inside. It appeared to be the closet of the adjacent apartment. He unleashed his revolver, "Carter, stay with Williams; Slater, come with me." He stepped inside. Once inside, he stopped and listened for any noises or movements. Slowly he slid the closet door open and peered inside. The bedroom was dimly lit but he was able to make out the figure of a woman lying in bed.

He stepped aside to allow Slater to enter, "Shhh...there's a woman in the bed," he whispered.

He slowly slid the closet door open and scanned the bedroom for anyone else. She was alone. Not knowing what to expect, Joe kept his gun pointed toward the woman as he cautiously made his way toward her.

"Donna?" he gasped when he recognized who it was.

Her eyes were closed and there appeared to be no signs of life. He put his finger on her throat, searching for a pulse.

As soon as Joe touched her, her eyes flashed open and she stated, "Hi, honey."

Caught off guard, Joe retracted his hand and stumbled backwards. "Oh shit," he gasped, trying to catch his breath. When he had regained his composure, he pulled the covers back exposing the woman's body, she was completely naked.

"This isn't Donna, it's a mannequin."

"A mannequin?" Slater questioned as he lowered his revolver. "Are you okay?"

Joe nodded although his heart felt as though it would explode. "Let's see what else is here."

He opened the bedroom door and stepped into the front room where he stopped and began sniffing the air. It was the same smell he had detected in the other apartment, only much stronger. Slowly and cautiously they searched the rest of the apartment. The kitchen area resembled a home made lab and the counter was cluttered with glass beakers containing a fleshy colored solution and one chocolate colored solution. Next to the beakers were several plastic containers containing what looked to be make-up kits used by actors and make-up artists, also on the counter sat several wigs on Styrofoam heads.

After determining no one was in the apartment, Joe holstered his gun. Inside the refrigerator were more beakers containing the same fleshy colored solution. Joe then opened the freezer. "Ahhh shit," he groaned.

"What is it?" Slater asked, looking inside. "That bastard," he said as he unconsciously began rubbing his wrist.

Joe reached inside the freezer and removed five plastic bags, each containing a human hand.

"What in the world was he going to do with these?" Slater asked, wincing as if imagining the pain each victim must have endured.

"Don't even go there," Joe answered. "Make sure Randy takes photos of these. Tell Williams I need him, and have Carter find out who this apartment belongs to," he said as he began putting the hands back into the freezer.

Joe was in the midst of studying several photographs that were pinned to a wall in the front room when Slater returned with Randy and Williams. "Randy, take photos of the packages inside the freezer. When you're done, Williams will pack them in ice and take them to the coroner's office. Notify Latent Prints and have them meet you there," he ordered.

Williams looked bewildered; he opened the freezer and looked inside. "You want me to pick those up and take them to the coroner's office?" he sputtered, a disgusted look on his face. "Lieutenant, I think I would be of much more value here. I can get a Black & White to transport those things."

"Williams, they're not going to bite. When Randy's through, take them to the coroner's office," he said sternly.

Williams reached into the freezer and touched one of the plastic bags, and then quickly retracted his hand.

"Oooh…Lieutenant," he gasped, his whole body shaking; "I really don't want to do this."

"Slater, would you mind helping Williams, Williams is apparently allergic to anything cold."

Slater chuckled; and when Randy had finished he placed the frozen hands inside a cooler and iced them down.

"Now Williams, you are capable of taking them to the coroner's office, aren't you?" Joe asked.

"Uhuh, but I want you to know I still don't like it," he said with a long sad face.

Joe looked at Slater; Slater was on the verge of uncontrollable laughter. "Get going," he instructed Williams.

Joe and Slater returned to the front room to further examine the photos on the wall. Each victim's picture was pinned, and under it was the newspaper clipping telling of their murder. Below the victims pictures were pictures of Murdock, Joe, and Mayor Walsh. On each photo, mathematical graphic gridlines were drawn with notes giving dimensions of their head, forehead, nose, ear, and eye. "What is this guy up to?" Slater asked.

Joe was perplexed, unable to answer.

When Joe had decided what he might tell the reporters, he went out to give them his promised statement.

"Lieutenant, we understand from a reliable source that you now know the identity of the killer of Barry Snider and the four other victims," one reporter suggested as cameras began rolling.

"Last night," Joe began, "we received an anonymous tip that the suspect in our serial killings was residing at sixty-four-fourteen Lexington Avenue. A search warrant was obtained and a search of the premises was made. We have found numerous items of evidence, evidence that clearly leads us to believe that this was in fact his residence. I cannot, however, go into what kind of evidence we have retrieved at this time, nor can I tell you the identity of the suspect, but as soon as I have confirmed the information we have obtained I will let you know. That's all I can say at this time, and I want to thank you in advance for your cooperation."

"Lieutenant, do you feel an arrest is imminent?"

Joe paused, "Let's not put the cart before the horse. We have worked hard and systematically on all information we've received. Today we have recovered some very encouraging evidence; however, it will take time to evaluate each piece. I'm not going to tell you that we're about to make an arrest, but I will say we are much closer. And when we do find him, we will have enough evidence to prosecute."

"Lieutenant…"

"I'm sorry; I cannot give you any further information." Joe turned and walked back into the apartment.

"And there you have it; police have finally gotten some...and as Lieutenant Norris put it, some very solid evidence. And very soon, they may just know who's doing these heinous killings that have plagued our city. This is Murray Fredericks...live from sixty-four-fourteen Lexington Ave.

Chapter Twelve

Joe was massaging his back as he climbed the stairs leading to his office, the pain was caused by an old injury he had sustained while riding the sand dunes of the Mojave Desert in a supped up dune buggy with his old buddy, John Hanna. They had just arrived for a weekend of fun, the sun was quickly disappearing and after their long trip, they couldn't wait until morning. So in they hopped, and with sand flying, up the nearest dune they climbed. They ascended the nearest crest and were cruising at a respectable thirty-five mph when they turned into the shadow of a near-by gully, instantly they were airborne and came crashing into the side of the sandy mountain like a bolt of lightning. Joe was momentarily knocked unconscious and John sustained a broken finger, both front tires exploded during the impact and their dune buggy was buried to the axle. When they failed to return, a search party was formed and they were quickly found. Within the hour they were on their way to the hospital, Joe on his knees with his chest lying on the front seat with torn ligaments in his back, while John drove with a broken finger.

"Good morning, Lieutenant, what a mad house," Sharon said picking up a ringing phone and cupping her hand over the mouthpiece, "Captain Murdock is in his office and wants to see you, right away."

"Thank you," Joe replied.

"Special Task Force Investigator Wilson," she said into the phone as Joe continued down the hallway.

Joe stopped in front of Murdock's office and knocked on the door, "Come in," Murdock said in his usual low craggy voice.

Murdock must have read Joe's expression as he eyed all the recovered surveillance items lying on his desk. "It's okay, we found them all," he said, a grin finally cracking his formidable face. "Every phone had been bugged, now that we can talk freely, what did you find?"

Joe took a deep breath, "The guy is extraordinarily complex and extremely intelligent. I know they say every criminal wants to be caught and on the surface it appears as if this is the case, but I have a gut feeling he only wants us to think this."

"Why do you say that?"

"Does it make sense," Joe asked, "for him to give us his address? I think it's a set up and he's toying with us like a cat with a mouse. He even has the audacity to call us on our own equipment and tell us we've overlooked a secret door that will lead us to the lab where he makes all of his disguises, and then he leaves prints like he's made them for us. Why would he do this?"

"He could be getting tired of running; do you have a problem with that?"

"Yes, I do," Joe continued. "I think he's trying to tell us something."

Murdock raised his hands in the form of a gesture, "What in the Hell is he trying to tell us?"

"We found a life size mannequin of Donna Forrest."

"You found what?" Murdock asked leaning back in his chair and pondering what Joe was saying. "Tell me more."

"At first I thought it was actually Donna," Joe said wide-eyed. "She appeared to be dead, so I put my hand on her throat to see if I could find a pulse. When I did, her eyes opened and she started talking. Joe shook his head, "I almost wet my pants," he confessed. "It turned out to be a mannequin, but it looked exactly like Donna down to the smallest detail, and I mean smallest detail," he reiterated.

"Do you think he's some sort of pervert?"

"I think he has some crazy delusion about Donna, and she may lead us to him."

Murdock leaned forward, "And what do you propose?"

"Since Robert is helping us, I want to show him the mannequin and see if he has any ideas. He's stalking Donna, and if Robert has no objections, I want a female undercover officer inside the Meadows. We have to protect Donna anyway, so why not let her help us catch him."

"It sounds risky but I don't see any other alternative, do you?"

Joe shook his head, "He's boasting that he's going to have Donna, and I think in his own sweet time he'll come for her."

"Do what you have to do, you have my complete authority. Anything you need, you'll get."

"Thank you, Captain."

"Did you show the mayor the photos that were found?"

"Yes; and he was very appreciative that you let me be the one to show him."

Murdock nodded his approval.

"I also advised him to have twenty-four hour security for him and his wife."

"Good. That's all we need is for him to wind up another Barry Snider," Murdock stated bluntly.

Joe nodded, "Anything else, Captain?"

Murdock replied with vengeance in his eyes, "Yes, let's get that son-of-a-bitch."

"This is Joe Norris, is Dr. Forrest busy?"

"He is but he should be finished in about fifteen minutes, I can have him call you?"

"Tell him I'll be in my office." Joe hung up and then dialed Hollywood vice.

"Lieutenant Jones."

"Warren, this is Joe Norris, I have a favor to ask."

"What do you need?"

"I need Dot Heron and one of your best men."

"Dot's working with John Harper, and he's one of our best. I can have them in my office in an hour."

"Good. Let me know when they get there."

"Would you like me to send them over?"

"It might be best if I come over there."

Just as Joe got off the phone, Carter called out. "Joe, Doctor Forrest is on line two"

Joe nodded, "Robert, how're you doing?"

"Surviving. Anything new?"

"Any chance you might stop by after work, I have some things I'd like to discuss with you."

"Sure, but before I forget, SID went through my house like a vacuum cleaner, every phone had been bugged.

"That explains how he's getting his information," Joe said not believing how much ground the suspect had covered in such little time. "I'll see you later."

Joe could hear Slater and Williams conversing in the hallway, and by the time he met them, they were in one of the interrogation rooms and had placed most of the confiscated evidence from Lexington onto one of the tables.

"Everything's been printed," Slater assured Joe. "But Williams has some startling information concerning the Donna doll," he said mysteriously as Williams left to retrieve the doll.

Joe picked up a glass beaker containing the fleshy looking substance and put it up against his arm.

"Looks real, doesn't it?" Slater remarked.

"It sure does," Joe replied, thinking of Murdock's impersonator as he sat it back on the table. He picked up one of the wigs and began scrutinizing it, the hair was long, matted, and dirty, "This fits the description Angel Martinez gave us of the killers hair," he said searching for a label. "See what we can find out about these wigs," he suggested.

"I've already checked each one; none have any labels or identifying marks. I thought I'd stop by some of the studios later and see what they might know."

"Good idea," Joe agreed.

"Excuse me," Williams said as Slater stepped out of his way. Williams laid the Donna doll on the table and removed the wrappings.

"Williams has come across some astounding piece of evidence," Slater remarked.

"Okay Williams, what is it?" Joe asked.

"Well," Williams said in an obviously uncomfortable state. "Is it stuffy in here or what?" he asked as he began loosening his tie.

"Williams," Joe snorted.

"Okay, okay. I don't want anyone to get the wrong idea, but when I picked the doll up I must have accidentally brushed against one of her breasts," he said squirming uneasily.

"Okay, Williams, what did you find?" Joe asked sternly.

"This…" and Williams reached over and reluctantly touched the doll's right breast. "Oh Robert, that feels so good. Please don't stop." The voice sounded exactly like Donna.

"Joe smiled and shook his head, "I already know she talks."

"There's more, Lieutenant," Williams continued, his face beginning to flush. "When one breast talked, I wondered what the other might say."

Williams touched the other breast, "Oh Robert, I love it when you do this to me."

"Is that all?" Joe asked still not amused.

"Not quite," Williams replied. "Now remember this is a murder case, and we must do whatever is necessary to get information, even if it seems to be to a little odd or extreme."

"Williams, what's the point to all this? Let's get on with it," Joe demanded.

"Okay, Lieutenant, now listen what she says as I touch her ahhh…pubic area."

Williams then touched the doll's pubic area and a man's voice growled within, "If I ever catch you touching Donna here, I will…" and then the voice began chuckling softly, "you know what I will do and you'll be alive to watch. I'll choose the time and place, and then

I'll take Donna from you just like you took my Joanie from me. One night you'll awake, and your eyes will be filled with terror but you'll not be able to scream. You'll want to turn and run but you won't be able to move." The voice chuckled again, "And you will watch as I slowly take your tongue in my hand…and then you'll scream no more."

Joe stepped back, "Whew," he said as a cold chill crept up his back. "That sure as Hell gives us something to think about. Book the other evidence but not the doll just yet. Doctor Forrest is on his way and I want his opinion."

"Okay, boss," Williams replied.

"Don't let any of this evidence out of your sight, I want one of you with it at all times," he said pointing to each of them. "Even if your best friend walks in, do not leave this room unguarded, do you understand?"

"Yes, sir," Williams shot back.

"Good work, Williams," he said trying not to laugh, but even he couldn't keep from chuckling as he left the room.

"Joe, Lieutenant Jones just called and said Dot Heron was in his office."

"Thanks, Montehue; call me when Doctor Forrest arrives."

Joe crossed the street and entered the Hollywood Vice building.

"Back here, Joe," Lieutenant Jones called out.

"What's up?"

"Like I said earlier; I'd like Dot Heron for an assignment."

"What kind of assignment?"

"A very dangerous one, that's why I wanted to talk with you first, if you don't think she can handle it, I won't ask."

"Why Dot?"

"Because she's had experience as a security officer in a mental institution."

"What do you have in mind?"

"Do you know who Doctor Robert Forrest is?"

"Isn't he the psychiatrist helping you with the serial murders?"

Joe nodded, "The killer has taken a personal vendetta against the Forrests for helping me, and he's done things to cause his wife to have a nervous break down."

"And what is it that you want Dot to do?"

"We have every reason to believe the suspect's next move is to break into the sanitarium, and we feel Donna's life is in jeopardy."

"And exactly what part will Dot play?"

"I want to plant her inside the sanitarium as a patient; she'll room with Donna and provide protection."

"Well…" he paused. "I think Dot is quite capable of handling it, however, it will be her decision."

"That's the only way I'll have it," Joe insisted.

"And what exactly will John do?"

"I need someone to act as her husband, someone who can come and go as a legitimate visitor and be able to transfer information at the same time."

"Would you like to ask, or shall I?"

"You can, but I have to know now. If she shows any interest, then I'll explain the details."

"Let's bring her in."

Jones opened the office door, "Dot, I need to talk to you." He held the door open as Dot entered and closed it behind her. Dot was a tall slender woman with short auburn hair, and she held her shoulders back with an air of confidence. Her healthy outdoor complexion made her look more like a professional tennis player than an undercover officer."

"Have you met, Lieutenant Norris?"

"I've seen the Lieutenant around, but we haven't met formally. Nice to meet you, Lieutenant," she said extending and shaking Joe's hand.

"Lieutenant Norris is in dire need of a female undercover officer, and he feels you might be the one that can get the job done. It's a very dangerous assignment and therefore strictly a voluntary one. If you're not interested, please feel free to say so."

Dot's eyes widen with anticipation, "What kind of assignment is it?"

"Joe, would you mind explaining what you have in mind?"

"First, I want you to know this is a very dangerous assignment, and second, there will be no pressure, if you're not interested tell me," Joe said bluntly.

"What is it?" Dot asked nervously.

Joe proceeded to explain the predicament the Forrests were in and what part she would play, should she decide to help.

"In other words, you're asking me to live inside the sanitarium."

Joe nodded, "And for your own safety, no one will know who you are except the administrator of the hospital. If you decide to help us, John Harper will pose as your husband and he'll be visiting you on a regular basis to transfer information to and from you."

"How long will I be in the hospital?"

"I don't know," Joe confessed.

"Can I take my gun?"

Joe shook his head, "That might be too risky; however, your room will be monitored twenty-four hours a day. We have enough evidence to believe the suspect will try and kidnap Donna, and I realize I'm asking a lot but her life is in immediate danger. I wish I could give you more time to make up your mind or that we had more time to prepare you for the assignment, but we don't. If you're not interested, I'll understand, but if you say you'll do it there will be no turning back. We have no time for cold feet, so think carefully before you answer, but I do need to know now."

"Ohhh…" Dot said closing her eyes and clasping her hands as if asking for a divine answer, and then as if all her questions had been answered, her demeanor returned to that of a confident professional. Her mind was made up and all doubts were cast aside, "I'll do it."

"Are you sure?" Joe asked.

"I'm sure."

"Sergeant Montahue is in charge of the operation, he will be coming over in a few minutes to fill you in on all the details. You and

Harper will follow him to the Sierra View Hospital. From there you'll be taken by ambulance to the Meadows Sanitarium. Remember, no one other than Doctor Shilling will know who you are, not even Donna. I want you to know I'm proud of you for your decision and we'll do everything we can to keep you safe. We will have policemen on the grounds, but don't get into any situation that you can't get out of by yourself."

Dot nodded, "I understand."

"Joe," Montahue called out as he entered the office. "I've gotten a fax from Latent Prints," he said shaking the papers he was holding. "They came up with a match."

"They did?"

Montahue nodded and handed Joe the papers.

"All right!" Joe shouted exuberantly.

"Hello," a voice called from behind. "Joe, it's me,"

"Bob, come in," he said cheerfully.

Joe turned to Montahue, "Dot Heron and John Harper are at Hollywood Vice, fill them in on all the details, I don't want any problems."

Joe then turned to face Robert, "I'm glad you could make it."

Robert was puzzled by the happy expression on Joe's face, "Good news?"

Joe nodded, "But there is bad news also, which would you prefer first?"

"I could use some good news, right now," Robert said passively.

"Then we'll start with the good news. Last night we received information that our suspect was living in an apartment on Lexington Avenue and that Judge Miley had signed a search warrant. We raided his apartment and found evidence galore, including a good set of prints. A match just came in from Latent Prints and we now know the suspect's name." Joe handed the report to Robert.

Robert began reading out loud, "The prints are a perfect match to those of Edward Bryant Pierce."

"Here comes the interesting part, look at the next page," Joe said.

Robert turned the page, "Homicide Report?" Robert asked looking very confused.

"Read it," Joe urged.

"Victim-One: Pierce, Edward Bryant, DOB: two-fourteen-forty-two, Male Caucasian, six-one, one hundred eighty-five pounds, light brown hair. "Officers investigation revealed that due to the residence being completely burned to the ground, it is unknown how the suspect may have gained entry. But according to the LAFD's investigation, the fire started in the master bedroom, where both bodies were found burnt beyond recognition. The Coroner's investigation revealed that death was caused by a blow to the head of both V-One and his wife, V-Two (Pierce, Joan Rachel DR# eight-four-eight-six-four-four). V-One's right hand was missing. Dental records taken by Dr. Arthur Jenkins were used to establish the identity of both victims. It is unknown at this time if any property was taken."

"What?" Robert gasped. "How can this be, this guy's dead!"

"Don't you see," Joe stated. "He's not dead, he's still alive. The body that was recovered had to be someone else. He must have made up fraudulent dental records and then assumed another identity."

"That could be possible," Robert agreed. "The date of the murder was April fourteenth, nineteen eighty-four. Have you gone to the LA Times to see what was written?"

"I'll be going in a few minutes, would you like to go?"

"Sure."

"But first, Bob, the bad news."

"Oh yeah, the bad news, I almost forgot."

Robert followed Joe into the interrogation room, "Will you excuse us for a minute?" he asked Williams.

"Sure, excuse me," he replied.

"I have something I must show you, and I don't know how to do it other than being direct. It's very sick, but I need your opinion," Joe said trying to be as compassionate as possible.

"Okay," Robert replied, never imagining what he was about to see.

Joe reached over and pulled the cover off the doll's face.

"Donna!" Robert gasped as his knees buckled.

"No, it's not Donna, it's a mannequin. We found it in the suspect's apartment."

Robert was in shock and unable to make a sound.

"Bob, are you okay?"

Robert nodded, "Just let me catch my breath."

"I understand, but there's more. Shall I continue?" he asked.

"Go ahead."

Joe pulled the cover completely off, exposing its naked body in its entirety.

"Oh shit, I think I need to sit down."

"I'm sorry, Bob, but I don't know of any other way to do this," Joe apologized.

Robert took several deep breaths, "I'm okay," he said as he continued his deep breathing.

"When I first saw the doll I thought it was Donna, too," Joe explained. "I couldn't tell if she was dead or alive, so I reached over to take her pulse. When I touched her neck, her eyes opened and she spoke to me…about scared me to death. Anyway, we found by touching her in different areas, she would say different things."

Robert looked at Joe, "I can't believe this is happening."

"I know," he said sympathetically, and then he reached down and touched her right breast, "Oh Robert, that feels so good. Please don't stop."

"Oh my God, that's Donna's voice," he gasped.

Joe nodded, "Okay Bob; now listen when I touch the left breast."

"Oh Robert, that feels so good. I just love it when you do this to me."

Robert stared at the floor, "He's sick, he's really sick."

"Bob, I have one more I want you to listen to, and I want you to listen to this one very carefully."

Robert looked up at Joe and shrugged his shoulders, "Let's have it, it can't get any worse."

"It is Bob. What he has to say is very disturbing and very frightening, actually it's a warning."

"What do you mean, a warning?" he asked mystified.

Joe then touched the doll's pubic area, and Robert listened as a man's voice growled from within. He turned pale and began wheezing unable to catch his breath.

Joe tried to console Robert, "Its okay, but I have to know if you've ever heard that voice?"

Robert nodded, "Lately, I've been waking in the middle of the night…and someone is standing over me with his hand in my mouth and he's grasping my tongue; that's the voice I hear."

"Whose voice is it?"

Robert shrugged.

"Would you like to hear it again?"

Robert immediately shook his head and began holding his stomach, trying not to vomit.

"Bob, yours and Donna's lives are in grave danger."

Robert looked into Joe's eyes, his face filled with frustration, "I've done everything I can, I don't know what else to do. Excuse me; I need to use the restroom."

Robert entered the lavatory, turned the cold water on and splashed some onto his face. "What am I going to do?" he asked looking in the mirror and watching the water dripping from his beard, and pondering how much he had to lose should anything happen to Donna. His insides ached to the point of nausea, and he was annoyed with himself for being so helpless. When he felt he had regained his composure, he returned to where Joe was waiting.

"What does this Donna doll tell you about our suspect?" Joe asked.

Robert paused for a moment to collect his thoughts. "It tells me that his wife must have committed adultery and he's blaming me for it. He thinks I'm responsible for him losing his wife and he's using Donna to get even. He has a complete fixation with her, and his fixation seems to be getting stronger." Robert paused to wipe the perspiration from his forehead, "He'll do anything to have Donna...even kill me if I try to stop him."

"That's my opinion also."

Robert covered his eyes with a wet handkerchief.

"For her protection, I've taken the liberty of placing a policewoman inside the sanitarium; she'll assure Donna's safety. Sergeant Montahue is coordinating the plan. John Harper, a vice cop, will act as her husband. I don't want anyone other than you and Doctor Shilling knowing who she is...for her safety as well as Donna's."

"You want to use Donna as a guinea pig?" Robert snorted.

Joe took Robert by the shoulders, "We have no choice, Donna's life is in danger and I want someone there to protect her."

Robert shook his head in disbelief.

"I know Doctor Shilling is a personal friend, so I want you to make sure Donna and Dot Heron are in the same room. Also, I want this audio-video pen placed in their room so we can monitor their every move. And I want Schilling aware of the gravity of what's going on, it could be a matter of life or death?" He then handed Robert the pen.

Robert nodded, "You're right, you're absolutely right. Believe me; I'll make sure he does what you want."

"Dot Heron will be transported to the sanitarium tomorrow," Joe continued. "I have to stop by the LA Times tonight, if you don't feel up to it, I understand."

"No, I want to go."

They could see the beer bellied security guard standing in the lobby as they approached the large plate glass door. "We're closed?" he stated and turned to leave.

Joe pulled out his badge; "I need to use your archive computer."

"Our normal hours are from eight AM until four PM, if you'll come back in the morning I'm sure they'll be happy to oblige you," he stated through the locked door,

"I don't have time for this," Joe snorted, his fuse short and about to explode. "I need to use your computer and I need to use it, now!"

The security guard began scrutinizing Joe's face, "Aren't you in charge of the serial killer investigation?"

Joe nodded.

A big grin appeared on his face, "Damn, why the Hell didn't you say so?"

Joe and Robert followed the security guard down to the basement where he unlocked a heavy door and swung it open.

"The computer's in here," he said switching the lights on. "I'm sorry about before," he apologized. "You can use this one," he said pointing to one of several computers.

"Thank you," Joe answered waiting for the security guard to leave. "We'll let you know when we're finished."

"Oh sure, right, I'll be out front," he sputtered. "Just let me know when you're done so I can lock everything up."

Joe turned the computer on and the LA TIMES ARCHIVES insignia appeared in large bold letters. Underneath was a box with the word Date. Joe typed, April fourteen, nineteen eighty-four and hit Enter. The Monitor flashed and instantly the front page appeared.

Joe began scrolling down the page until he came to a picture of a large mansion completely engulfed in flames, and beneath the picture was a picture of a man and a woman with the names, Dr. Edward Bryant Pierce and Mrs. Joan Rachel Pierce. The headlines read: *COUPLE DIES IN FIRE.*

"This is it," Robert whispered as they began reading the story.

"A fire broke out in the exclusive hillside of suburban Brentwood early this morning. Firefighters could not contain the raging fire that took the lives of two of the cities most prominent citizens; lost in the blaze that completely consumed their residence and left it in mere ashes were forty-two year-old Dr. Edward Bryant Pierce and his thirty-six year-old wife, Joan Rachel Pierce. Fire Marshall Lionel Dobson is quoted as saying, "We are looking into this matter as being the work

of a possible arsonist. It burned much too quickly and far too hot for a common residential fire and we feel some type of chemical may have been used to ignite the fire." Police are unable to give any motive for the murder of the Brentwood couple and are calling it a homicide due to the fact that Dr. Pierces' right hand had been severed and missing. Dr. Lee of the Coroner's office stated it was unlikely that either Dr. Pierce or his wife was alive when the fire started due to the fractures found in both skulls. Dr. Lee also confirmed that the bodies were burnt to the extent that dental records had to be used to positively identify the two victims. Dr. Pierce was one of our most brilliant and gifted citizens, having attained the unparalleled IQ of two hundred and forty. To put that into perspective, Albert Einstein had an IQ of one hundred and sixty. Dr. Pierce was a member of the prestigious Mensa Society which accepts only members with an IQ in the highest two percent category. Dr. Pierce held a PhD in Orthopedic Surgery and Plastic Surgery, as well as a Bachelors and Masters in psychology. Dr. Pierce is survived by his identical twin brother, Gary Bryant Pierce. Mrs. Pierce is survived by her two brothers, James Berman thirty-eight, and Ronald Berman thirty-three. Funeral services are to be held in Forrest Lawn Cemetery on Thursday."

Robert's face looked as though he had seen a ghost, "Holy shit," he gasped. "Do you realize who this is? He's a super genius! I can't believe this, he was an icon. He wrote several books on psychology, one, Reflections of Your Inner Self was considered a must for psychology students and is still widely used today."

Joe was thwarted and felt nauseas because of it. He was beginning to realize the magnitude of what he had just read; it was like trying to catch a great white shark on a twelve-pound test line or a hungry polar bear with a butterfly net.

He requested two copies, and the printer responded.

Joe picked them up and handed Robert a copy.

Robert began studying the picture of Joan Pierce, "The woman's face is very familiar, but the name Joan Pierce doesn't ring a bell. I think I'll go through my archives and see if she was once a patient."

"Let me know if you find anything," Joe answered, pondering what steps he must take now that he knew something about this...Dr. Edward Bryant Pierce.

Chapter Thirteen

Joe climbed the front steps of the old Superior Court building; its eloquent European style was grandeur in its day but was now showing signs of losing the battle of time. There were rumors the city of Los Angeles was thinking of tearing it down and it being replaced with a new modern structure, and although having only been built in the early 1920's, what stories its old walls would be taking to the grave. It was here on April twelfth, nineteen thirty-five that the city of angels had to decide whether law and order would prevail or continue to be terrorized by the influx of eastern gang lords. Judge Reginald P. Thomas, known for his strict enforcement of the law seemed to be the only one standing between its frightened citizens and the corruption of the mob. It was on this date that he sentenced Lawrence "Dutch" Logan and William "Mad Dog" Martin to die in the electric chair for the gangland style execution murders of six members of an opposing gang. They were fighting each other for control of the downtown area and its illegal drug operations, bookmaking, and prostitution rings. It was this conviction that created the enormous wave of public outcry to banish the mob and thus end their ruthless reign of terror. The trial lasted for months and reporters came from all over the country to cover its brutal story, however, Judge Thomas stood firm in his beliefs that good would prevail over evil, even after numerous attempts on his life.

Like greeting an old friend, Joe rubbed one of the cornerstones of the courthouse for good luck, something he had done for over twenty years.

"What floor?" a man asked as Joe stepped into the elevator.

"Second."

The elevator jolted upward as it strained to make its sluggish ascend. The lights began flashing as it neared its destination and the entire elevator began shaking violently as it rumbled to a sudden stop. Joe chuckled as he stepped from the elevator, feeling that once again he had cheated death.

Joe read the hand carved numbers imbedded above the old massive oak door as he entered the courtroom. Judge Orin Miley was seated on the bench and a Burglary trial was in progress.

Judge Miley gave no more than a quick glance as Joe entered and continued listening to the District Attorney question the police officer as to what probable cause he had for detaining the suspect, searching and retrieving evidence from his person, and subsequently arresting him.

Joe scanned the courtroom for an empty seat and sat down. When the District Attorney had finished asking all the questions pertinent for a conviction, he turned the police officer over to the Public Defender.

"Before the Public Defender begins questioning this witness," Judge Miley announced, "we will take a thirty minute break. Court is adjourned until eleven o'clock."

Judge Miley motioned for the bailiff to approach the bench. "Have Lieutenant Norris meet me in my chambers," he ordered.

The bailiff motioned for Joe to meet him at the bar, and then escorted him to the rear of the courtroom. "Lieutenant Norris is here, your Honor."

Joe entered the judge's domain, "Thank you, your Honor, for seeing me on such short notice."

"Have a seat," he said pointing to a well-worn leather couch.

Joe gave the judge the affidavit seeking a warrant be issued allowing him to exhume the grave sites of Edward and Joan Pierce.

Judge Miley began reading, "Its says you received a warrant to search the residence at sixty-four fourteen Lexington Avenue, and upon searching that residence you found several fingerprints and other evidence, which you confiscated. It also states that I signed the Search Warrant, do you have that warrant with you?"

"I do, your Honor," Joe replied handing it to the Judge.

Judge Miley scrutinized the Search Warrant and the authorizing signature. "It certainly looks like my signature," he quipped. "But as I told you earlier, I never signed any such warrant for Captain Murdock."

"I understand, your Honor;" Joe replied uneasily. "And as I tried to explain over the phone, I really don't know what's going on..."

"Well I certainly don't know what's going on either," Judge Miley interrupted, "but I do know it's going to take a lot of convincing for me to sign this affidavit."

"And I can appreciate that, your Honor, but what I do know is that someone who looked just like Captain Murdock came into my office and handed me this Search Warrant and said you had signed it. We spoke for over fifteen minutes and never in my wildest dreams did I ever imagine it was anyone other than Captain Murdock. The next day I told Captain Murdock of the search and he denied any knowledge of it."

Judge Miley listened with intensely as Joe continued his story.

"I also know that someone who looks just like me checked out almost all of our surveillance equipment and signed my name. I've known the officer in SID for over fifteen years and he swears it was me who he released the property to."

"Are you saying there may be more than one suspect?" Judge Miley asked.

"I believe there's only one suspect, your Honor, because the MO is exactly the same in each crime. Plus we've retrieved evidence from Lexington Ave. that also suggests there is only one suspect, items such as wigs, makeup, and artificial skin, indicating the suspect has the ability to disguise himself. He was certainly good enough to fool me," Joe confessed. "He apparently has the ability to forge signatures also, because if you didn't sign this warrant, your Honor, then he must have."

Judge Miley nodded, "Go ahead, I'm listening."

"When we searched the apartment on Lexington, we overlooked a secret door that allowed the suspect to escape. When I got back to Captain Murdock's office, he called us on the surveillance equipment that he checked out in my name. For some reason it was more important that we find this evidence than it was for him to hide the fact that he had bugged every phone in our office and had set up visual equipment to monitor our every move. He then told us to go back and continue our search, because we overlooked the secret door."

"He did what?" Judge Miley blurted, not believing what he was hearing.

"I'm not sure why he's doing this, but I do know he's a brilliant man and is always two steps ahead of us. It's gotten to the point that he calls to tell us where his latest victim can be found. He's got to be stopped, your Honor. When I served the search warrant, I served it in good faith because I thought it was Captain Murdock who gave it to me, and God as my witness; I had no reason to believe that it was signed by anyone other than you."

Judge Miley pondered for a moment, "In all my years, I've never been involved in a case as strange as this. You do realize that this puts me in the middle of a rock and a hard spot. The only reason I'm going to sign this affidavit is because I have known Captain Murdock for more years than I can remember, and because I have such great admiration for you. I do realize we have to get this guy off the streets, but it does us no good if we can't keep him off. I hope you realize the evidence you confiscated was seized illegally and cannot be used against him in a court of law."

Joe nodded, "I do, your Honor."

"Okay, partner," he said taking a pen and signing the affidavit, "Go dig um up."

Robert made a beeline for the back room where his archive files were kept. He opened the drawer labeled M-R, but found no patient with the name of Joan Pierce. Thinking it may have been misfiled, he began sorting through the rest of the files but he was still unable to find a file under that name.

Robert removed the copy of the LA Times from his pocket and began studying Joan's picture. Then the last paragraph in the clipping struck a memory cell, Joan Pierce is survived by her two brothers, James Kerman thirty-eight, and Ronald Kerman thirty-three.

He sat letting the information sink in. "Kerman...Joan Kerman, now that rings a bell," he said slamming the drawer shut and opening the appropriate drawer. He began sorting through the files until he came across Joan Kerman's file.

He returned to his office and opened the file: Joan Rachel Kerman. DOB: January eight, nineteen forty-eight. Spouse: Edward Bryant Kerman. Address: two-five-three-seven-seven Glenwood Circle, Brentwood, Ca.

"Why did she say her husband's name was Edward Bryant Kerman when it was Edward Bryant Pierce?" He began scanning the file and picking out the meat from his intensive studies as page after page brought back recollections of his sessions with Joan Pierce, AKA Joan Kerman. Robert had always prided himself on his astute ability to take comprehensive notes, and this only confirmed his beliefs.

February third, nineteen eighty-four:

This is my first session with Joan; she appears to be very timid and clasps her hands nervously when she speaks. She is very concerned about our Doctor/Patient privileges and wants to be assured that I will not discuss any issues with her husband. I advised her that everything we discuss is strictly confidential. She says her husband treats her like a child and acts more like a father than her husband. She relates that although they have a beautiful home, it feels more like a prison than her sanctuary...

February tenth, nineteen eighty-four:

Joan appears to be very nervous when she speaks of her husband, he is very strict and overly protective and she is being smothered in their relationship. She relates that she sometimes wakes up in the middle of the night from a bad dream and she's in a cold sweat and unable to breathe...

February seventeenth, nineteen eighty-four:

Joan continues to be very nervous and says she doesn't know which way to turn, she wants more freedom in their relationship but each time she tries to address her feelings, it always ends in an argument...

February twenty-fourth nineteen eighty-four:

Joan is becoming more confident, but her husband feels threatened by her want of independence and they are having more squabbles than ever...

March third, nineteen eighty-four:

Although Joan has her Associates Art Degree, she is expressing a desire to take an evening art class at a local college. She is tired of being alone, but her husband rejects the idea...

March tenth, nineteen eighty-four:

Joan is continuing to express her desire to begin an art class, the next one being in mid-April. She says it will take away her loneliness. She relates that her husband has lost any desire for a sexual relationship. She is reluctant to say why...

March seventeenth, nineteen eighty-four:

Joan has finally confided that her husband is impotent; she fears it is due to his extensive work hours and he becomes irritable when she approaches him intimately. She teases him by saying that I (meaning me) would not push her away if she were to approach me. She tells him she has a crush on me and often dreams we are having an affair. She has met a young man, an artist by the name of Danny Morris, and although she says their relationship is purely platonic, the two are seeing each other occasionally...

March twenty-fourth, nineteen eighty-four:

Joan relates her husband is becoming more suspicious, possessive, and abusive. He feels the reason she is seeking independence is because I am telling her she has the right to her own identity. He feels I am responsible for his wife not loving him because I'm filling her head with these crazy ideas. She's using me as a wedge, and she appears to be vaguely aware of how using me like this reflects her ambivalence toward me, another doctor. She's not ready to explore the transference, though.

She is finally admitting to her affair with Morris, and it is such an arousal for her, knowing that they are making love in his bed and Jacuzzi. But she shows no remorse for her husband thinking it is me who she is having the affair with...

March thirty-first, nineteen eighty-four:

Joan's right eye is bruised, but she insists it happened when she accidentally fell during an argument.

April seventh, nineteen eighty-four:

Joan's lip is swollen, and she now reveals that her husband has beaten her twice and seems to enjoy inducing brutality, both verbally and physically. His anger is now elevated to rage, and he's threatening to stop by my office and confront me concerning my adulteress ways. She warns me to be very cautious if he does, because he has become obsessed with punishing me. She said this all began as a harmless prank to console her loneliness, but has since become very frightening and she is going to leave him...

April fourteenth, nineteen eighty-four:

Joan never showed up for our session, I tried to contact her but her phone was disconnected. I stopped by the address she gave, but no one seems to know her...

For the first time, there seemed to be a light at the end of the tunnel. He picked up the phone...

"Joe, Doctor Forrest is on line-two," Slater called out

Joe waved, "Bob, what can I do for you?"

"I've found out why Pierce is stalking me."

"You did, why?"

Robert went into all the details of his findings so Joe would have full knowledge of what had happened.

"That certainly clears up a lot of questions, what's the chance of getting a copy of your sessions?"

"Joan and Edward are both legally dead, so our doctor/patient confidentiality ceases. If you can stop by tomorrow, I'll have a copy for you?"

"I'm exhuming the remains of Edward and Joan in the morning, I'm not sure how long it will take but I'll stop by as soon as I'm through. You know this could mean Donna's life is in even greater danger than we thought. You are making sure you're not being followed when you visit her, aren't you?"

"I'm positive, if there's any question I just keep driving until I am."

"How's she doing?"

"Better, but she still wants me to pull strings so the hospital will let her wear her wedding ring. I would order another one, but I'm afraid she'd know the difference."

"Your insurance company should have a photo, why don't you check with them."

"That's a great idea. By the way, I'm really impressed with the security at the Meadows; it sure takes a heavy burden off my mind."

"I'm glad you feel good about it. Listen, I've got to go but I'll see you tomorrow, and thanks for the information."

"Joe;" Slater hailed. "SID called while you were on the phone; they've finished analyzing the fleshy substance in the glass beakers. They said it contained components that can easily be purchased across any counter, but what was really impressive was the unique way each component fused with the other. They said the composition is quite ingenious and that it would take someone with an extensive chemistry background as well as the use of a complete laboratory to complete such works. Also, the beaker containing the chocolate substance contained the same pigmentation of an African/American, and that might be the answer to the missing janitor. They'll be sending a memo specifying exactly what each component is."

"You could be right, make sure a copy gets into our file."

"Will do," Slater replied.

Montahue parked his unmarked police vehicle in the Sierra View Hospital parking lot while Harper drove directly to the emergency entrance. Harper was assisting Dot from the car when Montahue and a nurse arrived pushing a wheelchair.

"What seems to be the problem?" the nurse asked as she began assisting Dot into the wheelchair.

"My water broke and I'm about to have my baby," Dot replied, almost in hysteria.

The nurse looked down at her flat stomach, "How many months pregnant are you?"

"Nine," Dot replied.

The nurse looked at her skeptically. Montahue stepped forward, looking as if being a little embarrassed, "I called earlier and gave all the information to Doctor Johnson."

"Okay, let's take her inside," the nurse said as she wheeled Dot toward the emergency entrance.

The entrance doors opened revealing a room filled with patients waiting to be seen by a doctor.

"I'll get Doctor Johnson," she said hurrying to the nurse's station.

"Doctor Johnson, Doctor Johnson, please come to the emergency room," she broadcasted over the loud speaker.

In a matter of moments, a female doctor rushed to the nurse's station, a short conversation ensued and Montahue saw the nurse pointing toward them.

The doctor hastily approached, "I'm Doctor Johnson, we have a room waiting for you."

"Which room do you want her in?" the nurse asked.

"Take her to Room Five, put her on the table and take her vitals. I'll be right there."

After the nurse had taken Dot.

"I'm Janis Johnson, an old friend of Joe's," she said in almost a whisper. "Joe told me what was going on and asked that everything we do tonight look authentic. I have an ambulance ready to transport Dot to the Meadows Sanitarium. We'll give the nurse a few minutes to get Dot's vital signs and then we'll go inside, you can stay with Dot while I notify the ambulance."

Montahue nodded.

Dr. Johnson led Harper and Montahue to Room Five, "How's her vital signs?"

"They're well within normal limits; however, she seems to be experiencing severe abdominal pain."

"I'll take it from here," Dr. Johnson stated as she unlocked the medicine counter and removed a vile and syringe. She stuck the needle into the vile and removed a small portion of liquid. "I'm going to give you a little shot; it will help ease your pain." She doused Dot's arm with alcohol and quickly injected the needle.

Dot watched the needle pierce her skin and the liquid quickly disappear from the syringe.

As soon as the nurse was gone, "What was in that?" Dot asked.

"Don't worry, it was only sterile saline. Just lie back and I'll get the ambulance attendants, they'll transport you to the Meadows Sanitarium. Good luck," she said patting Dot on her shoulder.

Dr. Johnson then left the room.

"Any questions before they get here?" Montahue asked.

Dot shook her head. "But if anything should happen, I want you to tell my mother I love her and that I wish I could have been with her on her birthday."

"Nothing's going to happen," Montahue replied as a lump began forming in his throat. "When's her birthday?"

"Next week, she'll be seventy-six," she said brushing tears from her eyes.

"Next week! Don't you worry, you'll be back way before that!" he said forcing a smile. "Harper and I will make sure of that."

Suddenly the door burst open and two men wearing white medical uniforms rushed in pushing a gurney.

"Hi," one said softly. "We're going to move you onto this gurney and we'll try not to hurt you. Are you ready?"

Dot nodded.

They lifted her from the table and placed her onto the gurney, "That wasn't bad, was it?"

Dot shook her head.

"If you're ready, we're going to take a little ride."

"Wait," Dot shouted, reaching out for Harper's hand.

The attendant stopped, "If you'll stand right here," he said pointing to a spot next to the gurney, "you'll be able to hold her hand."

Harper moved to the spot and Dot nervously took his hand.

"Are you ready, now?" the attendant asked with a big smile.

Dot nodded.

"Okay, here we go," he said as he began pushing the gurney out of the room. "You can come with her if you'd like."

"I'm sorry, sweetheart, but I'll need to follow you in my car," he said giving Dot's hand a gentle squeeze.

"You are coming to the hospital, aren't you?" she asked.

"I'll be right behind you."

Harper continued holding Dot's hand until they raised her up and slid her inside the ambulance.

Montahue watched as Harper ran to his car, caught up with and followed the ambulance out onto the street.

The ambulance stopped in front of the Iron Gate, security officer Terry Austin exited the guard shack and approached the driver's side.

"Who do you have, Mel?"

"A female with an Alien pregnancy, she's overdue and might deliver at any time," he said snickering and making motions that she was a loony. "She's having a mental breakdown and Doctor Johnson requested she be brought here. Here's our authorization signed by Dr. Shilling," he said handing Terry the paperwork.

"Are you working with, Tom?"

"Yes, and that's Dot Heron's husband is in the car behind us."

Terry looked toward the car and its blinding headlights. "Wait here," he said walking back to Harper's car.

"Can I help you?" he asked as he shined his flashlight inside the car.

"I'm her husband," Harper replied pointing to the ambulance.

"Back up fifty feet and turn your lights out, after the ambulance goes through the gate I'll signal for you to pull forward but do not move forward until I tell you to."

Terry walked back to the guard shack and entered the number of the ambulance, time, driver's name, attendant's name, and the patient's name in his log. He returned to the ambulance and opened the rear door, peering inside.

"How're you doing, Tom?"

"Pretty good, Terry, how about you?"

"Not bad," he said closing the door and walking back to the guard shack. He pushed a button and the massive iron-gate began moving aside until the road was cleared.

After the ambulance had passed, the gate immediately closed. Only after the ambulance had reached a certain distance, did Terry motion for Harper to move forward.

"Can I see your ID, please?"

Harper handed him his California driver's license.

Terry studied Harper's driver's license, "If she's your wife, why is your last name different than hers?"

Harper smiled, "We just got married and haven't had time to change it."

"I'll need to get authorization for you to enter, if you're who you say you are, it shouldn't take long. Stay in your car," he ordered and headed toward the guard shack. Terry picked up the phone.

"Nurse Fleming."

"This is Terry at the front gate, I have a man who says he's Dot Heron's husband."

"What's his name?"

"John Harper."

"The last name is Harper?"

"Yes, he said they were just married and they haven't had time to get her ID changed."

"Let me check; yes, here it is. Dr. Shilling has authorized it, you can let him in."

Terry motioned for Harper to move forward and the gate began to open. He returned Harper's drivers' license and gave him a guest pass. "Follow this path until you come to the main building, on the left is a parking lot, park there and go straight to the Admittance building. Be sure to wear your guest pass at all times and do not go anywhere else."

Harper nodded. "Talk about tight security," he thought as he drove pass the gate.

He scanned the parking area, security cameras were everywhere. He followed the well-lighted path that took him straight to the Admittance building; there he was met by two muscular medical attendants.

"Can I help you," one asked.

"My wife was in the ambulance."

"What's her name?"

"Dot Heron."

"And yours?"

"John Harper."

The attendant looked a little skeptical as he began looking through a stack of papers, "Here it is, you're only authorized to be in this area," he warned. "Dr. Shilling likes to meet the spouse of each new patient; I'll let him know you're here." The Attendant pressed Dr. Shilling's speed dial number and a short conversation ensued. "Doctor Shilling is expecting you, this way please."

The attendant escorted Harper to Dr. Shilling's office, where he knocked soundly on the door.

"Come in."

The attendant opened the door; "Mr. Harper is here."

"Thank you, Gary; you may go. I'm Doctor Shilling, and you must be John Harper?" he said shaking his hand.

"We'll need to go over a few things concerning your wife," he said as he motioned Harper to have a seat. Would you like some coffee?"

"Yes, black please."

Dr. Shilling poured a cup and handed it to Harper.

"You run a tight ship."

"Yes we do, and we have to. I'm the only person in the hospital that knows who you and Dot are, and for her safety I must keep our relationship strictly professional."

"I am very impressed with your security, you have a good man at the front gate, he's very thorough."

"That means a lot coming from you," he complimented. "I'll show you to Dot's room and give you a few moments alone. Did you bring the surveillance pen?"

"I did."

"At exactly eleven o'clock, I'll cause the guard who monitors Dot's room to leave his post; it will only be for a moment so you'll have to move fast. I'm going to let you place the surveillance pen in the position you feel it will best serve its purpose. Are you ready to go see your wife?"

"Yes, I am."

Chapter Fourteen

The parking lot was full of activity; men were scampering about readying their equipment while others were already amidst interviews and shooting footage of the cemetery office and surrounding grounds. As soon as his car came to a stop, reporters quickly gathered, clamoring for that strategic position in which to ask their sea of never ending questions.

"Why that bastard," Joe thought, "he's done it again."

"Lieutenant...Lieutenant," each hailed trying to be heard above the other.

Joe raised his arms in an attempt to bring some sort of order to the relentless group. "Gentlemen, please. I've asked you to meet me here," he said reluctantly, and knowing reporters were the last thing he wanted to deal with at this time, "because I feel we've finally gotten the break we have been hoping for. Our suspect has made a fatal mistake and we have recovered a set of his prints. Our suspect's name is Dr. Edward Bryant Pierce. We ran his name through our records, NCII and the FBI, and found that he was named as the victim of a homicide on April fourteenth, nineteen eighty-four."

"Joe...Virgil Thomas, KNXT TV. I'm a little confused as many of my colleagues apparently are. If this Dr. Pierce was the victim of a homicide in eighty-four, then how can he be a suspect in these killings now?"

"That's a very good question, Virgil. Two bodies were found when the LA Fire Department responded to a fire that completely burned Pierces' house to the ground. Both bodies were burnt beyond recognition and the coroner had to rely on dental records for identification. But now, we have conclusive evidence that indicate the dental records may have been fabricated. Until it is proven otherwise, it is our opinion that Dr. Pierce is still alive."

"In other words, Lieutenant;" Virgil continued, "Doctor Pierce may have killed yet another person?"

"Yes, and that's why I've received authorization to exhume their grave sites. When we get the results from the DNA and can determine whose bodies are in fact in these graves, I will personally let each of you know. But for the time being, I'm asking a favor," and then he paused long enough to make eye contact with several key reporters. "I have given you all the information I can at this time, and out of respect for those who have loved ones here, I ask that we not turn this into a spectacle. I would greatly appreciate it if you would go about your business and let us do ours. I thank you for coming."

Joe got into his car and slowly drove toward the grave sites of Edward and Joan Pierce, looking into the rear view mirror he could see the reporters gathering their equipment and loading them into their vans.

Upon reaching the location, he stopped to read the words inscribed on the tombstone, "Dr. Edward Bryant Pierce, born February fourteen, nineteen forty-two. Died, April fourteen, nineteen eighty-four." And just below on the same tombstone was another name, it read, "Joan Rachel Pierce, born June twenty-four, nineteen forty-eight, died, April fourteen, nineteen eight-four."

The cemetery personnel had spread out large rolls of heavy black plastic on the area next to the grave being excavated and had a miniature backhoe standing by. Three men were in the process of cutting the sod, rolling it up, and placing it upon the black plastic. After the sod had been removed, the backhoe operator began the unholy task of excavating the site. He raised the bucket and gently sat it down precisely where he wanted to begin digging, his fingers moving with the grace and precision of a pianist as the bucket quickly and steadily dug into the sacred ground.

He repeated the process of digging and piling the dirt until he had removed exactly five feet of soil, at which time he swung the bucket over and sat it on the ground. Two men then climbed into the hole and began removing the remaining dirt until the entire casket was completely uncovered. They then slid a braided nylon line under the head and foot of the casket and gently began raising it with the backhoe. As the casket cleared the hole, Joe could see the remaining casket below.

The backhoe operator swung the casket over to the rear of a black Hearse; two men brushed off the remaining dirt and then slid the casket inside. The same process was performed on the second casket; during the whole ordeal not a single word was spoken.

"I'll meet you at the cemetery office," Joe instructed the driver of the Hearse, breaking the silence.

Joe took the time to survey the cemetery, it looked so peaceful and serene, yet each tombstone told the painful story of tragedy and suffering and the loss of someone's mother, father, son or daughter. He was unable to understand how a doctor, a healer, a man of medicine could turn into such a cruel sadistic cold-blooded killer.

Joe signed the necessary papers giving him custody of the remains and the right to remove them from the cemetery grounds. He gave the driver of the Hearse copies of his authority and instructed him to take the caskets to the Coroner's office.

"Where's that little imbecile off to now," he asks sarcastically as Robert's car leaves his office in a direction other than home. His eyes begin to sparkle when he realizes his patience is about to pay dividends. "I know where you're going, now take me to her," he says in a low cynical whisper.

Using his GPS Tracker, he etches Robert's every move in his memory. He watches as Robert turns off Sunset Blvd. onto Duff Place, his vehicle makes a sharp right turn and moments later come to a brief stop. Then it moves several hundred yards and appears to park.

"I guess it's time we take a little ride and see the country side," he said amusing himself. "Oh, a hunting we will go…a hunting we will go…hi ho a dairy-o…a hunting we will go…The doctor finds his wife…The doctor finds his wife…

"Hi, honey, how are you feeling?" Robert asked.

Donna reached over and took her husband's hand; "Much better. Everyone is being so nice, but I can't stop worrying about you."

"You're worrying about me, that's just like you," he smiled. "You're making so much improvement…I can't begin to tell you how happy I am."

"Oh I almost forgot, I have a new roommate," she said turning to Dot. "Dot, I want you to meet my husband, Robert."

"Hi, Robert; it's nice to meet you."

"Nice to meet you, too. I can't tell you how glad I am that Donna has a roommate."

"She's been so much company," Donna said with a gleam in her eye as she pulled Robert close and whispered in his ear, "She thinks she's pregnant by an Alien," she said cupping her hand over her mouth trying to scuffle a soft giggle.

The man retraced Robert's route until he came to a stone wall, but instead of turning right as Robert did, he turned to the left and pulled his car off the roadway and hiding it amongst the trees and foliage. He followed the narrow road until he came to the guard shack, and in the protection of the shadows, he crept onward until he could see the security officer inside. He waited for the appropriate moment and then moved silently until he was standing next to the window. Hanging on the wall inside, was the entire list of patients authorized to enter that evening, and another list contained the names of all the employees, their position and extension numbers.

Suddenly a flash of headlights appeared, and he quickly moved into the protection of the shadows until the vehicle came to an abrupt stop in front of the Iron Gate.

As the security guard did his routine check of the ambulance, the man quickly entered the guard shack and placed a bugging device into the telephone. Then he quickly memorized all the names, addresses, work and home phone numbers of Dr. Schilling, the four doctors working the night shift, their work schedules, the night-head nurse's name and phone number, the number to the Admissions Department, and the phone number to the guard shack as well as the authorization forms of all the incoming patients. And then like a thief in the night, the man vanished, the unsuspecting guard never aware of his presence.

Joe flashed his badge into the video camera, and instantly the gate opened. Joe waved to Miles as he passed, found an empty space in the subterranean garage and parked.

"Good afternoon, Lieutenant," Miles said with a big smile as Joe entered the lobby.

"You look happy, is everything okay?" Joe asked.

A confused look crossed Miles face momentarily, and then a big smile reappeared, "You got me that time, Lieutenant."

"Keep an eye on my Porsche, will ya," Joe asked with a straight face as he headed toward the elevator.

Miles looked over at Joe's car, "If that's a Porsche, Lieutenant; then I got me a Rolls."

"Remember, beauty is in the eyes of the beholder," he said with a quick wink before stepping into the elevator.

"Hi, Lieutenant," Carol said looking at her watch.

"I know I'm early."

"Oh that's okay; Doctor Forrest will be finished in a few minutes. Would you like a cup of coffee while you wait?"

"Please."

"You take cream and no sugar, right?"

"You do have a good memory, and I understand your son is a gifted athlete?"

Carol cocked her head to one side and began chuckling; "Did Doctor Forrest tell you that?"

Joe smiled.

"I guess I'm just a proud mom. Yes, for a four-year old he's quite an athlete, especially at baseball. You should see him hit the ball," she said beaming.

"Enjoy the moment, it goes so fast," Joe said thinking of his own son and daughter.

The door opened and Robert's patient waved to Carol as he left his office.

"You can go in now, and you can take your coffee if you'd like."

"Hey Joe, I'm glad you could stop by. How did every thing go?"

"It's a little soon to know, but it was certainly interesting," he replied.

"How's that?"

"I've tried keeping this whole thing under raps so the press wouldn't get wind of it, at least until we got the results from the DNA. But when I arrived at the cemetery I was bombarded by reporters, and they knew exactly why I was there." Joe shook his head, "None of this makes any sense, he's our best witness, and most of our evidence has come from him. It's like he's forcing our investigation down the path he wants us to take."

"Pierce is a genius, that's for certain," Robert reinforced. "And if he's half as intelligent as I know he is, he's thought out every detail well in advance. It's as if we are playing a game of chess, and we are his sacrificial pawns moving in whatever direction he chooses. Unfortunately he's the king, and he's waiting patiently to swoop down and devour us whenever the urge arises," Robert remarked.

"That's spooky," Joe confessed. "But I also know that there's no such thing as the perfect crime."

"Well, let's hope this isn't the first," Robert replied, somewhat less than confident of that old cliché.

"Do you think he's giving us information because he wants to be caught?" Joe asked.

"Pierce is definitely not your ordinary murderer…and none of us has ever had to deal with a criminal of his stature before. I think he's giving us the symptoms he wants us to have. So far it seems to be that of a criminal who wants to be caught, or of a criminal who thinks he cannot be outwitted." Robert shook his head, "I'm not sure either is correct. I think it goes a lot deeper than what we see on the surface, but what I am sure of is," and Robert paused for a moment, "that in his mind he already knows how this will all end."

Joe studied the deep concerned look on Robert's face, "That's pretty eerie, Bob."

Robert nodded. "After I spoke with you yesterday, I made a copy of all my sessions with Joan Pierce." Robert opened a drawer and began thumbing through his files. When he could not find the file, he went through them again. Joe could see frustration mounting as he went through his files for a third time.

"I don't understand it, I put the file right here. I'm sure of it."

He picked up the phone, "Carol, have you seen my file on Joan Kerman?" he asked nervously.

"No Doctor, I haven't."

"Humph," he sighed. "Thank you."

"She hasn't seen it." There was a moment of eerie silence. "He's been in my office, I know it," he said his face turning pale. "Maybe Miles saw something," he said picking up the phone.

"Security, Miles."

"Miles, this is Doctor Forrest, has anyone been in my office after my going home last night?"

"Let me check, Doctor Forrest."

Robert could hear Miles shuffling papers, "Doctor Forrest?"

"Yes, Miles."

"I don't see any notations, and the cleaning service wasn't here because they come on Sundays and Wednesdays."

"And you didn't personally see or give anyone permission to come into my office?"

"No sir, I certainly did not!" he replied emphatically.

"Did anyone come into the building after hours?"

"Nobody came in after business hours, is something wrong?"

"I'm just missing one of my files, thank you anyway."

"I have to tell you, Joe, I'm about at the end of my ropes. Nothing seems to stop this guy, neither security alarms nor guards." Robert began stroking his beard as he pondered the situation; "Miles' desk is right in the middle of the lobby on the First Floor, anyone going to or from my office would have to walk right past him. How can this be?" he asked.

Joe shook his head, "I don't know, but somewhere there's a logical explanation."

Robert thought for a moment, "You're right, we have to keep things in perspective. Even though he's a genius, he's still just a man and can only do what a man can do."

"I'm relieved to hear you say that, I was beginning to wonder if we were up against some kind of supernatural being," Joe said jokingly.

"Well in some ways he is…intellectually speaking anyway," he said somberly.

"Don't do that, Bob," Joe said shaking head. .

"Buzzz!"

"Yes, Carol,"

"Your next patient is here,"

Chapter Fifteen

D octor Gucci's on line-one" Williams called out.
Joe waved and picked up the phone, "Doctor Gucci, good news I hope?"

"Yes and no, the bone was in very bad condition but we were able to conclude that cause of death in both corpses was due to their Parietal and Temporal bones being crushed. The instrument used was very hard, possibly a bat or something very similar. One corpse was a male and the other was a female, but the male was not Edward Pierce."

"Any idea who it might be?"

"Not at this time, but we do know he was a Caucasian in his thirties, about six feet tall."

"At least that gives us a place to start, anything else that I should know?"

"He had an amputation at the right wrist."

"Like all the others?"

"Exactly."

"How about the female?"

"It was Joan Rachel Pierce."

"Was her hand missing?"

"No."

"Now we have our motive, I appreciate all your help."

"My pleasure."

"Williams," Joe called, motioning him to his desk. Joe handed him the information received from Dr. Gucci, "One was Joan but the other wasn't Edward, we need to find out who it is. Joan was having an affair with a Daniel Albert Morris; find out everything you can about him, also see if a Missing Person's Report was taken on him on or around April fourteen, nineteen eighty-four."

"Will do."

"Joe," Slater called out, "Mr. Wesley Hamilton is on line-two,"

Joe nodded, "Danny my friend, how is the best defense attorney in California doing?"

"Hey Joe, Cheryl and I was just talking about you and Cole last night. Sounds like you're closing in on the serial killer, are you about to get'um?"

"We're closing in," Joe chuckled, "but this guy's slipperier than Houdini."

"I just wanted to let you know we're all behind you and…Joe, I'm sorry someone just came in and I'll have to call you back, but after you catch this guy, let's get together for dinner."

"That sounds good, Dan, keep in touch." Joe sat for a moment pondering how long it had been since he had talked to his old navy buddy, his was like a voice from the past and pleasant memories flourished. But his train of thought was broken when Slater approached holding a nineteen sixty-six UCLA yearbook.

"I stopped by the campus and looked through their archives; this is the year Edward Pierce graduated. If you'll turn to page forty-five," he said handing Joe the book, "you'll see that Pierce was voted Most Likely to Succeed. The article mentions his girlfriend at the time, a Nancy Baker. I've researched Nancy Baker and found she's now Mrs. Frank Shepherd. I called Nancy Shepherd and she confirmed that the two were almost married and would be happy to discuss Edward Pierce with us."

"What time are you to meet her?"

"In about forty-five minutes."

"I'd like to go, if you don't mind?"

"I was hoping you might say that."

Joe stood up, "Okay partner, you're driving."

176

Slater drove west/bound on Sunset Blvd. into the city of Beverly Hills, he took a tree-shaded street that ended in a cul-de-sac, on a mailbox at the very end was an address, and it read twenty-six forty-two Milborne Place.

Slater turned onto the driveway leading to the house above.

The house was sitting on the side of a hill; its manicured grounds had a park-like setting and a pristine white Rolls Royce sat under an open carport. They found the doorbell amongst the ornate carvings that proudly displayed their family crest. The chimes rang to the melody of "It's a Wonderful World" and it seemed to play most of the song before the door was finally answered.

"Can I help you?" asked a middle-aged woman wearing a suspicious look on her face.

"We're here to see Mrs. Shepherd," Slater replied.

"And whom may I say is calling?" she asked in a very dignified tone.

Joe removed his badge from his pocket, "Mrs. Shepherd is expecting us."

"Oh," she said putting her hand over her mouth and stepping backwards. "I...I'll tell her you're here," she stammered. "Please, come in."

She hastened into the kitchen and opened a door leading onto a patio in the back yard.

They watched as the maid approached a silver-haired woman sitting under a colorful umbrella, a short conversation ensued and they could see the maid pointing toward them. The woman nodded and the maid returned to where Joe and Slater were waiting.

"Mrs. Shepherd would like you to join her in the back yard. She also asked if you would join her in tea."

"That would be nice," Joe answered.

"This way, gentlemen."

The woman looked up as Joe and Slater approached, "Good morning, gentlemen, I'm Nancy Shepherd, please have a seat?"

"Thank you, ma'am," they replied.

"Mrs. Shepherd, I'm Sergeant James Slater and this is Lieutenant Joe Norris."

"It's nice to meet you both," she said, giving each a hardy handshake.

"When I talked with you on the phone, you indicated that you and Edward Pierce were very close. Can you tell us a little more about him?"

"Oh my yes, we were very close. As I told you earlier, we were engaged to be married but why all the interest in Edward now?"

"We're investigating the homicide of…" and Slater stopped when he saw the woman's jaw go agape.

Mrs. Shepherd began studying Joe's face, and then she raised her hands to her trembling lips, "I recognize you, you're the one investigating those dreadful killings."

Joe nodded.

"Oh no!" she cried. "I've read what terrible things he's doing; do you think he killed Edward?"

"No ma'am, but we would like to know more about Edward," Joe injected.

"Oh my God, I loved that man. I guess after all these years, I still do. He was such a wonderful person, so brilliant…so funny…so gentle…so energetic…and so full of life," she said sadly.

"I've read that he was very brilliant," Joe said softly.

"Brilliant?" she countered. "You have no idea what brilliance is unless you knew him. Did you know that he had the highest IQ in the history of UCLA, and possibly the highest ever recorded? Did you know that he had a photographic memory, and if he read something one time he would never forget it," she stated proudly.

"You mentioned that he was a gentle man, can you expound on that?" Joe asked.

A smile lit up her face, "Gentle…why he wouldn't hurt a fly."

She froze momentarily, her eyes staring into space and her big beautiful smile sparkling as her mind once again traveled back in time to her precious moments spent with Edward, "We used to kid him about that. When we were walking and a spider or an insect would be in his path," she paused and smiled; "he would always walk around it...never step on it." She shook her head, "He wouldn't hurt anyone or anything."

"It says in your yearbook that he also took acting classes?" Joe asked.

"Oh yes...there wasn't anything Edward couldn't do. He had so many talents. Did you know that he was the most gifted baseball player our school ever had...And that he broke the school's rushing record in football, which still stands today...and that all the NFL teams were trying to sign him? His Dad was so angry when he wouldn't sign with the Rams," she chuckled.

"What kind of acting classes did he take?" Joe asked.

"Oh...drama, comedy, it didn't matter," she said as a matter of fact.

"What kind of costumes did the school use?"

Mrs. Shepherd couldn't control her laughter; "Our school supplied the costumes, and they were horrible...some we couldn't tell in what play they were to be used. But not Edward, somehow he made his own, and you wouldn't believe how realistic they were. I remember one day," she said chuckling to herself. "I came into the drama class and Mr. Whittaker, our teacher, was sitting behind his desk. We were early but he insisted that we start our rehearsal. Anyway, we were all on stage and Mr. Whittaker was going over everyone's part, and telling each student how he wanted their part to be played. Everyone was listening attentively to his instructions when the front door opened...and in walks Mr. Whittaker! We couldn't believe our eyes. Everyone looked at Mr. Whittaker on stage...and then at Mr. Whittaker at the front door. We weren't sure which the real Mr. Whittaker was. You had to be there to really appreciate his ingenuity and sense of humor, he was so much fun. I almost died when I read that he and his wife had been killed in that dreadful fire."

"Did you know Joan Pierce?" Slater asked.

"Not really," she replied sadly. "She was younger and we really never met. After they met, he had eyes only for her. That was one thing I truly admired about him. He was loyal, but he expected those he cared for to be loyal to him. He did have the decency to tell me of his involvement, although at the time I took it pretty hard and I guess I've never really gotten over him. I still cherish his memories," she said wiping the tears from her eyes.

"Mrs. Shepherd," Joe said standing up, "I want to thank you for taking the time to share your memories of Edward with us."

"You're welcome, but you haven't had your tea."

Joe shook her hand, "Next time, but we really must be going."

"I'm sorry, I didn't mean to be such an old wind bag," she said shaking Slater's hand. "And I want to thank you for coming," she replied graciously.

"Lieutenant; a Missing Person's Report was taken on a Daniel Albert Morris, and Doctor Gucci confirmed that he was the male corpse. I put a copy on your desk."

"I thought that might be the case," he answered, pleased that they were finally getting some breaks.

Joe picked up the report and began reading, *MISSING PERSON'S REPORT, April seventeen, nineteen eighty-four. Daniel Albert Morris, Male Caucasian, DOB, November-eleven-nineteen forty-five, 6'0, 180 pounds, brown hair, brown eyes. ADDRESS: eighteen twenty-four Laurel Canyon Blvd., Hollywood, Ca.*

PR (MP's mother) states that she last heard from MP on April fourteen, nineteen eighty-four at six PM just before he left home for work. Due to PR's health, MP calls her everyday and has done so for the past five years. MP is an art teacher at Los Angeles City College; he is single but has recently been going with an unknown female, possibly also a teacher at the same college.

Joe picked up a blank Crime Report and in the appropriate spaces wrote, Homicide, Daniel Albert Morris. He filled out the remaining portion of the report using the information he had acquired from Dr. Gucci as to the identity and cause of death. He attached the Homicide report to the Missing Person's report and put it in the bin to be sent to Robbery-Homicide Division at Parker Center for follow-up and notification of next of kin.

The waitress led them to an empty booth next to the window, "Coffee?"

"Please," Richard answered as he and Robert turned their cup upright.

"I've noticed you two boys coming in every Wednesday for quite some time," the waitress remarked as she poured their coffee. "You're both very interesting, you dress like lawyers but you can't be because neither of you is obnoxious enough. So my guess is, you're either doctors or own a computer business of some kind."

Robert began chuckling, "Are you analyzing us?"

She smiled, "It's a hobby. Some people like to paint, others like to garden. Me, I like to people watch. If I'm right, remember me with a generous tip?"

Robert nodded, "That's fair enough."

"You are both doctors," she said matter-of-factly.

"Your hobby is our profession," Richard replied.

"Really...you're psychiatrists? That's a doctor," she chuckled. "That explains your demeanor and why you always speak so soft and calm."

"Well thank you," smiled Robert.

"You're welcome, our special today is a pastrami sandwich on rye, potato salad and a culture pickle," she said handing Robert and Richard their menus.

"Hmmm. The special sounds good."

"Make it two," Richard injected.

After the waitress had gone...

"So now that you've had a couple months to analyze this mysterious doctor of yours, what are your feelings?"

Robert began chuckling, "He's extremely bright and obviously gifted, or at least that's what he says."

"What do you mean by that remark?" Richard asked.

"Before our conversation gets out of hand, I want you to know you're absolutely right. Dr. Morgan cannot be the killer because it's impossible for a person to be in two places at the same time. And even though their lives do parallel one another, there's no way he could have possibly done it," Robert said wanting to put an end to the discussion.

"How do their lives parallel?" Richard asked.

"For instance, both seem to have a classic Narcissistic personality and both feel far superior to all those around them. They feel their ideas are the only ones worthy of discussion and both feel their IQ far exceeds the norm."

Robert then leaned forward almost whispering, "Now this is where it gets even more bazaar; both went to UCLA and were both gifted athletes…both in baseball and football…and both were scouted by the NFL. Both of their fathers were big football fans and both wanted their son to sign with the Los Angeles Rams."

"Very interesting," Richard surmised.

Robert sat back and slowly stroked his reddish beard, "Now what are the odds of that being?"

Richard shook his head, unable to answer.

"Here you go," the waitress interrupted as she placed their food in front of them.

"Hmmm, that does smell good," Robert said, giving the waitress a quick wink.

"Enjoy," she replied chuckling to herself.

"Today," Robert continued as he picked up his sandwich, "Doctor Morgan told me that he plays several instruments, the piano, the sax…and the harp.

"The harp?" Richard said almost choking on his food.

Robert took a bite of his sandwich, "Yep, the harp, but no matter how strong their lives parallel one another, you cannot be in two places at the same time."

"Nope, that's a fact," Richard injected as he took a bite of his culture pickle.

"Not only that, but he was working the weekend we were in Santa Barbara."

"That would indeed be impossible, that is if it really was him working that weekend," Richard teased, a sly grin emerging.

Robert started to take a bite of his sandwich but stopped and looked at Richard, pondering the possibilities.

"Come on Bob, I was only kidding," he smiled.

Robert nodded, "Yea, I know." But what if it wasn't him, he thought.

Carol was at her desk when Robert entered, "How was lunch?" he asked.

"It was great," she said elated. "Mike brought Mickey and we all had lunch together."

"That's nice."

"Yes, it was," she shot back proudly and looking much like the perfect mom.

"Before sending Mrs. Beck in, get Doctor Morgan on the line."

Robert had no more than sat down when Carol buzzed.

"This is Doctor Forrest, is Doctor Morgan in?"

"I'm sorry, Doctor Forrest, but Doctor Morgan just stepped out."

"Do you know what time he'll be back?"

"He won't be back today; would you like to leave a message?"

"Yes, oh by the way, do you remember me calling a few weeks ago and your saying Doctor Morgan was on Call that particular week-end and that he even performed emergency surgery?"

"Yes, I do."

"Would you recheck the hospital log and verify that it was actually he who performed the surgery. It would have been the first weekend of March."

"Sure thing, one moment," and Robert could hear her sorting through several papers. "Doctor Forrest, I'm sorry, I must have given you some incorrect information."

"What do you mean?" Robert asked as the hair on the back of his neck began standing on end.

"The log I saw before showed Doctor Morgan being on call that weekend, but this log indicates that he and Doctor Taylor switched duty, and it was actually Doctor Taylor who performed the surgery. And I can't find the original log anywhere."

Robert's jaws tightened and he broke out in a cold sweat, he tried to swallow but the knot in his throat prevented it. "Never mind, I'll call him later," he uttered, his voice barely audible.

"I knew it!" he shouted, almost startling himself. He looked at the door half expecting to see Carol barging in. "I knew it," he whispered. "That's the only thing that makes any sense."

Joe picked up the phone, "Bob, what can I do for you?"

"I have some information you should know, remember when Donna and I went to Santa Barbara and there was a murder while we were there?"

"Yes."

"At the time I was completely convinced that the killer was a patient of mine by the name of Doctor Stanley Morgan, so when I got back to Beverly Hills I called him at work, he was not in but his nurse told me he had duty that weekend and even performed a surgery that normally takes several hours. When I heard this, I knew it couldn't possibly be him even though up to that time everything pointed to him."

"And now?"

"I just called the hospital and the same nurse told me that the log she had gotten the original information from had been replaced with another log, and this log stated that Doctor Morgan and Doctor Taylor had switched duty that weekend. Doctor Morgan was not at the hospital that week-end."

"What is Doctor Morgan's home address?"

"Twenty-six forty-three Robin Hood Lane. And another thing," Robert added. "I had a session with him this morning and he was unusually cool and arrogant, the way he cocked his head and looked at me, I had the feeling that he was taunting me for some reason. He didn't come out and say anything, just a mild undertone. At the time

I assumed that it was just his Narcissistic Personality Disorder coming out."

"I appreciate the information. I'll have Latent Prints compare his prints with those of Dr. Pierce. In the meantime, I'll put a stakeout on his house and watch his activity."

"I think that's a good idea," Robert confirmed. "I'll talk to you later, bye."

He watches as the two men prance around the table trying to out hustle the other in a five-dollar game of pool. The cigarette smoke is stifling inside the small neighborhood bar and the jukebox is blaring out a sad country song, but even so, he could still hear the man's loud arrogant voice above all the other distractions.

The player wearing the cowboy hat laid his smoldering cigarette on the rail of the pool table and began tapping his cue stick on the table in front of the ball, "This is one son-of-a-bitch I'm not going to miss," he boasts arrogantly. He clumsily strokes his cue sending the ball into the corner pocket with a loud thud. "Take that you little shit," he shouts drunkenly at the ball lying inside the pocket.

He takes a long swallow from the bottle of beer and turns toward the man he is playing, "What the Hell are you looking at?" he bellows with a scornful look.

"Nothing," the heavyset man says, shrugging his shoulders.

"You better not or I'll kick that fat ass of yours," he sneers.

The man sitting at the bar motions for the bartender to bring him another shot of Scotch. The bartender picks up the bottle of Black Label, fills a clean shot glass and puts it in front of him.

The man motions for the bartender to lean closer, "Who's the obnoxious one?"

"That's Jake Plummer; he's a mean mother when he's drinking. I have to call the cops every time he comes in, wants to fight everybody," he remarks as he begins wiping the bar down with his towel.

"Take him a drink," the man says softly.

"I don't think that's a good idea."

"Take him a drink," he orders.

"I hope you know what you're doing," he replies.

The man watches as the bartender sets the beer in front of Jake.

"What the Hell's this for?" Jake shouts.

He could see the bartender pointing in his direction, and Jake strutting toward him like a peacock with his feathers all fluffed.

"What are you, some kind of faggie queer," he smirks.

All conversations stop as the patrons' eyes turn toward Jake and the man.

"He's not a fag, Jake, he just wants to buy you a drink, that's all," the bartender says trying to sooth his ruffled feathers.

"He looks like fag to me," he scoffs.

But the man is unshaken and he doesn't even acknowledge Jake's presence. He merely picks his drink up and takes another sip as if not hearing Jake's remark at all.

"I asked if you were a fag," Jake bellows and reaches over to grab the man's shoulder.

The man turns to face Jake, and with lightening fast reflexes reaches up and grabs Jake by the neck and pricks him with a tiny needle attached to his finger. Jake's eyes bulge and his body freezes. Everyone is stunned; they were all expecting Jake to perform one of his grand scenes.

"Get him a chair," the man orders.

"What's wrong?" the bartender asks.

"I'm a doctor and I think he's having a stroke," he says as they help Jake into a chair. Doc shines a small flash light into Jake's eyes to see the reaction of his pupils. "He needs to go to the hospital; someone put him in my car."

"Sure thing, Doc," the bartender answers. "Harry, you and Tom take Jake to the doc's car."

Chapter Sixteen

The spotlight illuminated only a small area, the rest of the room is surrounded by blackness as if inside some dark and desolate cave. He looks into the mirror and sees his steel-gray eyes staring coldly back, he leans closer making certain nothing is being over looked and not a wrinkle out of place. Slowly and meticulously he puts the final touches on his make up.

"Ahhh, Doctor Schilling," he utters as he admires his incredibly lifelike work. "It's time you stop what you're doing and bring your wife home."

He stands up and claps his hands, and the lights flash on. Instantly the darkness is gobbled up and the faces of Lieutenant Norris, Captain Murdock, and Mayor Walsh can be seen sitting on their Styrofoam heads. He stops long enough to pat each on the top of their head, "Don't worry boys, I haven't forgotten you," he reassures them.

He pushes a concealed button and the wall closes, leaving no signs of the secret room. He strolls down the elegant cherry wood hallway and opens two massive doors that lead into the master bedroom. Once inside, he checks to make certain the oak bar used to secure the doors is in its place. In each corner of the room, sits two five-gallon containers filled with airplane fuel and two sticks of dynamite.

A man is lying on the floor in the middle of the room, only his eyes are able to move. In a futile attempt, he tries to scream as the man with the steel-gray eyes picks up a container and begins soaking the room. With the task completed, he kneels down beside the man on the floor. "What is going through that tiny little mind of yours?" he asks. "You don't look like the same person who spoke so bravely earlier, you obnoxious little bastard," he says as he begins patting him on the side of his face. "Remember your boasting of your affairs, and of the husbands who weren't man enough to confront you because you were such a tough son-of-bitch? Well, when you live by the sword you die by the sword, and speaking of dying, it's curtain time Doctor Pierce. Just lie there like a good little boy until I return." He raises the container and begins dousing fuel onto the man's body. "Gas gives the body such a wonderful tingling sensation, don't you agree?" He sits the empty container beside the man and takes one final look around the room, "I think it's time we bring this to a conclusion, don't you?" He then wipes his hands and tosses the rag onto the man's face.

He presses a stone incased in the fireplace and a section of the fireplace opens. He steps inside and follows the tunnel until he comes to another door. Pushing on another stone, the wall opens exposing a large room containing several urns. On one wall is a heavy iron door, he unlocks it and steps out into a park-like setting at the rear of his estate.

He follows a tree lined path that leads to the street below and gets into his car. He enters Dr. Schilling's address into his GPS and instantly a map of the city appears giving him the shortest route.

The house is dark with the exception of a single lamp over the front door, but there is sufficient light for him to see Dr. Schilling's car in the driveway. He drives past Schilling's house and parks down the street, and quickly returns on foot. He quickly hot-wires Schilling's car and backs out of the driveway, turning in the direction of the Meadows Sanitarium.

"Good morning, sir, is something wrong?" the security guard asks as Dr. Schilling's car comes to a stop.

"Something has come up and I want you to be especially careful tonight," he warns. "I want you to be on your toes, and if you notice anything unusual I want to be notified immediately."

"Yes sir; nothing will get past me," he replies confidently. "Do you want me to let them know you're here?"

Dr. Schilling shook his head, "Just open the gate."

Without further ado, Terry does as he is instructed. Dr. Schilling drives straight to the main building and parks in his private parking space.

"Good morning, Doctor Schilling, can I help you with anything?" one of the male attendants asks.

"As a matter of fact you can, wait at your desk until I summons you, because I'll need your help shortly."

"I'll be ready, sir."

Dr. Schilling steps into the elevator and pushes the third floor button.

"Doctor Schilling, is something wrong?" the nurse asks as he approaches the nurse's station.

"I'll explain in a few minutes, please wait here until I call you."

"Certainly, Doctor," she replies.

Dr. Schilling enters room three-thirty-two, and as he is approaching Dot's bed he removes a small needle from his pocket and quickly pricks her arm. Dot's eyes shoot open but it is already too late, her body is completely paralyzed. She tries to scream but nary a sound can be heard. She is helpless and can do no more than blink. Dr. Schilling hovers over her, sniffing the scent of her neck. With his face only inches from hers, he whispers, "I know who you are, and you know who I am. I should rip your tongue out but I have more important plans." Then his cold lifeless eyes turn toward Donna, and with the quickness of a cat he moves to her side, pricking her also.

"Wake up my sleeping beauty," he says as he removes a small velvet lined container from his pocket. He positions it so she can see and slowly opens it, exposing the wedding ring he had taken from her finger earlier. He lifts her lifeless hand and puts the ring back on her finger. "Now you are mine," he says as if a wedding had just taken place. "And you're going to be such a beautiful bride tonight."

He begins stroking Donna's hair and asks, "Are you ready to take a little ride?"

Dr. Schilling picks her up and places her into a wheelchair and wheels her to the nurse's station.

"I've received information that Mrs. Forrest's life is in immediate danger and I'll be taking her to a safe location. Have Gary meet me downstairs, and I want this kept as quiet as possible," he warns.

"Would you rather I get an ambulance?" the nurse asks.

"No," Dr. Schilling chastises angrily. "It's too dangerous, and don't ever question my authority again. Now call and make sure Gary is waiting!"

By the time the elevator reaches the first floor, Gary and a female nurse are waiting.

"Take Mrs. Forrest to my car," Dr. Schilling snaps.

Noting the tone in his voice, Gary does so without hesitation.

Dr. Schilling then turns to the nurse, "Remember what I told you."

As Gary is placing Donna into Dr. Schilling's car, he notices tears in her eyes. "Doctor Schilling, look she's crying."

A ray of hope emerges as the attendant tenderly brushes the tears from her cheek, but she is devastated as Dr. Schilling delivers his final blow, "If you only knew the position she's in, you'd be terrified too. Remember, for her safety I don't want a word to anyone that she has been removed from the hospital."

Gary shrugged, "Yes sir, you know best."

Joe turned the lamp on and quickly glanced at his watch; three-thirty AM. "Now what?" he grumbled, knowing that a phone call at this hour could only mean trouble. He picked up the phone, "Hello."

"Lieutenant, this is Paul Frazier, I'm sorry to wake you but I've just had some strange activity in the girl's room. Doctor Schilling came in and whispered something in Dot's ear, and then he went over to Donna and put a ring on her finger. Then he put Donna in a wheelchair and the two left.

"Can you see, Dot?"

"I can see her but she must be sleeping, because she hasn't moved."

"Damn, I can't believe it. Call the police, and keep an eye on Dot until I get there."

Joe quickly began dressing.

"Are the girls all right?" Colleen asked.

"I don't know, call Robert and have him meet me at the sanitarium."

As Colleen was dialing, Robert was picking up a ringing phone.

"Hello," Robert answered.

"Doctor Forrest?" the voice asked nervously.

"Who's this?"

"This is Nurse Hansen, I…."

"Nurse Hansen!" he interrupted, "Is something wrong?"

"I'm not sure, and I certainly don't want to alarm you," she replied. "But it seems rather odd for Doctor Schilling to be moving your wife by himself, especially if her life is in danger. And the attendant who put her in his car said she was crying."

"He did what?" Robert asked as his mind began filling in the blank spaces. "Are you sure it was Doctor Schilling?"

"Of course I'm sure; I've worked for Doctor Schilling for more than ten years."

Robert took a deep breath trying to control his anxieties, "When did he take her?"

"Just a few minutes ago."

"What's Doctor Schilling's home number?"

Nurse Hansen gave Robert the number, "But he'll not be home yet."

Robert quickly dialed the number, "Yes," an exhausted voice answered. "What do you want at this hour?"

"Charles, this is Robert Forrest," he stated, his voice audibly shaking.

"Robert, what's wrong?"

"Nurse Hansen just called and said you took Donna from the sanitarium."

"I did what? That's absurd," he snorted.

"Oh my God, he's got Donna."

"Who's got Donna?"

"Pierce, he came to the hospital impersonating you and took Donna," Robert gasped, knowing that his worst nightmare had just come true.

"I must go to the hospital and see what's going on," Dr. Schilling stated still not believing what Robert was saying.

"You do that; meanwhile, I'll call Lieutenant Norris and tell him what's happened."

All his life, answers to difficult questions came easy, but the feeling of uncertainty and loss of control was something new to him, and he didn't like it one bit. A large lump formed in Robert's throat as he was dialing Joe's home number.

"Joe, this is Bob, we got problems. Our boy's done it again, he's impersonated Doctor Schilling and has taken Donna from the Meadows," he said almost babbling.

"I know, I just got a call saying Doctor Schilling was acting strangely. Cole's been trying to call you but your phone's been busy. How's Dot?"

"She must be all right, they didn't say."

"I'm on my way to the Meadows; I'll meet you there in twenty minutes"

"Is Donna all right?" Colleen asked as Joe hung up the phone.

Joe shook his head, "Pierce has kidnapped her."

"Oh my God, no."

"Please be careful."

Joe nodded, "I'll call you when I know what's going on," he said giving her a quick kiss.

Colleen took a deep breath as Joe opened the drawer to his night stand and removed his Smith & Wesson snub-nosed revolver and placed it in its holster.

Pierce drives Donna from the sanitarium straight to his love nest in the Hollywood Hills, leaving the innocent world behind.

"And how's my little angel doing," he asks as he gently lifts her from the car and places her in a wheelchair.

"Shall I show you to our room, me lady? We would normally be staying in the master bedroom, but tonight we will be in the west wing," he informs her as he wheels her down the long elegant hallway to their room.

The bedroom is massive, imported Persian rugs decorate the hardwood floors, while luxurious cherry wood covers its twelve-foot walls, and surrounding the four-posted canopied bed are dozens of lighted candles illuminating the darkness, while the sweet scent of lilac permeates the air.

He lays her on a luxurious goose down bedspread and positions her so she can see the gift-wrapped package on the nightstand. "This is for you, my dear," he says as he opens the package and showing her a beautiful black negligee.

"I picked it out for this very special occasion...and now if you will allow me the honor," he asks as he begins removing Donna's hospital gown...

"You look so beautiful, black is definitely your color," he praises as he leans over and they exchange their first kiss. Now if you'll excuse me, I'll go change into something a little more comfortable," he says closing the door behind him.

Donna had no idea how long she lay there, but she did know the power of the drug had not diminished. Suddenly the bathroom door opens and a distinguished looking gentleman appears, he is tall and extremely good looking and is wearing a red smoking jacket. As he nears, she notices something oddly familiar and gasps when she recognizes him to be a much younger version of the man in the supermarket. In his arms is a silver tray, and upon the tray sits a carafe of red wine and two crystal glasses. He places the tray in the middle of the bed and sits down beside her.

"I hope this meets with your approval? I know it's one of your favorites and I want everything to be perfect tonight." he boasts proudly,

He smiles and chats continuously as if he were a young man on his first date and as if Donna were there by her own free will.

"I have something I want to read, it will enlighten you as to what your ex-husband is really like."

He walks over to an elaborate antique dresser and retrieves the file on Joan Kerman from one of the drawers and sits back down next to Donna.

"This is the file your filthy ex-husband did on my little Joannie. I took the liberty of removing it from his office and I've been waiting patiently for us to read it together so you'll know what a lying adulterous imbecile he really is. Now let me know if you can't see," he says as he continues his sick charade.

"Let's start with their first session; it was February the third, nineteen eighty-four. Your ex says Joan is nervous and wants to make sure that I, meaning your husband, will not violate our Doctor/Patient confidentiality. Their next session is February tenth," but instead of reading it out loud, Dr. Pierce begins scanning the session. "No, no; she's mistaking, I wasn't strict, I only wanted to protect her." Pierce continues scanning the page, "Ahh-haaa, here we are," he shouts jubilantly. "On February seventeenth he's trying to put it in her head to be more independent, and more of the same garbage on the twenty-fourth. And on March the third, they're talking about her wanting to take an Art class, and you can be sure it was his idea. And on March seventeenth...what's this?" he asks as he stands up and begins pacing back and forth. His face turns a bright red as he reads her accusation of him being impotent. "That's a lie!" he shouts angrily.

Donna holds her breath as Pierce becomes more and more irate, knowing he has all ready killed.

"What a liar he is, I was not abusive," he continues in his rage. "I loved her, but she was having an affair with your husband."

Donna watches as tears stream down his cheeks when he reads of his wife admitting to committing adultery.

"He's lying, he's the one who had the affair with my wife, I know he did," he shouts.

He sits down on the bed, not wanting to believe the truth that had just been revealed. He sees his reflection in the silver tray and angrily flings Robert's notes in Donna's face. He then snatches the tray up and violently throws it at a mirror hanging over the dresser, shattering it into a thousand pieces. Defeated, he falls to his knees, sobbing tears that had been bottled up for years.

"He's lying," he cries out as his head begins jerking spasmodically from side to side. "He took my life and stole my identity," he said whimpering like a lost child. "And now he's even messed this up, oh how I hate him," he snarls through gritted teeth as if trying to revive the madman within. Enraged, his cold lifeless eyes turn toward Donna, "Don't you dare look at me like that," he scowls as he takes a large pillow and angrily covers her face.

All of her life Donna suffered from claustrophobia and was unable to sleep with her head under the covers, and now she fears that is how she will die.

"I don't want you anymore," he scoffs. He storms into the bathroom and flicks the switch on and instantly the lights flash brightly as if he had just stepped onto center stage and is being hailed for a suburb performance. The crowd is applauding his entrance and his eyes sting as the multitudes of flashes sparkle in the darkness. He smiles, waving to his adoring fans as they shout, encore, encore, until he notices one lonely face staring sadly back. His jubilation is cut short as he feels himself being drawn toward the sad face by some mysterious force that is beyond even his understanding. He looks familiar, he thinks, cocking his head to one side, but tonight he refuses to dwell on any unhappiness and quickly turns his head only to have another appear. Then one by one all the happy faces begin to transpose themselves into the likeness of the sad face until there is not a single happy face remaining. He is completely surrounded by sadness and grief. Horrifyingly, the sad faces begin laughing and taunting him as they move closer and closer until he is completely encircled and can feel their hot breath on his face. Just as they are about to devour him an electrical current shoots through his body, knocking him to the floor. Like a defenseless child, he clasps his hands over his eyes until there is total silence, and then peering through his fingers, he begins looking about. When the room appears to be empty, he picks himself up. Suddenly the sad face reappears.

"You've been such a fool," the sad face hisses. "All these years, it's been you cheating yourself out of happiness. You were so brilliant, but you let your ego lead you into destruction," he said sharply. "Robert didn't have an affair with Joan."

"He did, I know he did," Pierce rebukes.

"You know nothing of the sort; you've just read the truth."

"What Robert said isn't true, or she would never have come back to me."

"She didn't come back to you, and she's not Joan!"

"She is too; can't you see they're exactly alike?"

"They look nothing like, you had such hatred for Robert that you chose to see her like that," he snapped.

"I did not."

"You did too, and don't lie to me, I was there."

Pierce reaches out and touches the sad face, his fingers sliding across the mirror. "Robert didn't have an affair with your wife; you know that now, don't you?"

Pierce nodded shamefully.

"What are we going to do?" the sad face asks.

"I'll divorce her," Pierce replies.

"She's not yours to divorce. What shall we do?" the sad face snaps.

"The only thing we can do," Pierce says looking into the eyes of the sad face, "you must die for what you've done."

"But I didn't do anything, you did. I don't want to die," he gasps.

"You must, one of us must die so the other may live."

The sad face's eyes fill with tears, "Why don't you die?" Then the sad face turns his back on Edward, "Go, I don't want you to see me like this."

"Burr its cold," Williams remarked as he pulled his knitted cap down and began rubbing his hands together trying to keep them warm. He glanced at his watch; four-thirty AM.

Williams poured two cups of coffee, their steam rising and fogging the windows. Slater took the time to wipe the condensation from the window before taking a sip. "Ummm that does hit the spot," he remarked, looking out onto the cold desolate street as the fantasy of a warm bed crossed his mind. "Its nights like this," he admitted, "that I wish I had stayed in teaching. I enjoyed working with my students, helping them explore their minds and solve unknown equations using known scientific data."

"Yeah right, I don't believe that for a minute," Williams interjected. "What you're really saying is that you would rather be home sleeping inside your warm bed, but I know better because as long as there's a murderer on the streets you're going to be a part of it, even if you have to be freezing your butt off with me all night."

"You do make it sound romantic," Slater chuckled.

Suddenly the dark clouds turned their ugly heads and hurled an assault of rain at them. Slater casually turned the wipers on, clearing the windshield. He looked at his watch, Six forty-five AM, normally the sun would be rising by this hour but the thunderheads had filled the skies and it looked like it was going to be a long wet day.

"We're getting movement," Slater announced, pointing to the garage as the door began rising. He picked up the mic, "Six-W-Ten, this is Six-W-Thirty-three."

"Go ahead, Slater."

"Joe, the garage door just opened and a car's backing out."

"Can you see who's driving?"

"Only that it's a man," he said looking through his binoculars; "What kind of a car is it?"

"A white Mercedes."

"Follow him, Six-W-Five will be waiting at Sherwood Forrest Place and Robin Hood Lane, he'll take over from there but stay close."

Pierce made a right turn onto Robin Hood Lane and 6-W-Thirty-three followed a short distance behind.

A few minutes later, he made a left turn onto Sherwood Forrest Place.

"This is Six-W-Five, I have him in site."

"Six-W-Thirty-three back off and let Six-W-Five take over."

"Six-W-Five, he's turning left onto Sunset Blvd."

"Six-W-Seven, when he comes by your location, take over," Joe ordered.

"Six-W-Seven, I have him in sight."

"Good, don't lose him. The rest of you, stay close but out of sight."

"Six-W-Seven, he's turning into the Sunset Plaza Hotel and he's parking just south of the main entrance. He's getting out of his car, he's wearing a dark full length raincoat and a blue hat and he's carrying an umbrella and a small red duffle bag."

"Stick with him; everyone else, make sure the building is surrounded."

"I'll be closer than a fart on a..." Montahue started to quip as he stepped from his car. "Testing, testing, can you hear me?" he asked into his pen radio.

"You're coming in loud and clear," Joe shot back.

"He's on foot and heading toward the front entrance."

Pierce walked briskly, not looking anywhere but straight ahead.

"He's entering the lobby and he doesn't appear to be aware of our presence," Montahue reported.

"Don't let him out of your sight, but don't crowd him either," Joe advised.

Montahue followed him into the lobby, "He's going inside the restaurant."

"Montahue and Brown go inside, everyone else surround the restaurant. You know what to do if we get the chance, but until then stay close and keep your eyes open. We don't want to lose him," Joe reiterated.

Montahue and Brown entered the restaurant and positioned themselves so they could watch his every move. A waiter handed Pierce a menu, he ordered and then he removed a newspaper from his duffle bag and began reading.

"It looks like we'll be here for a while; he's just ordered something to eat and is reading the paper."

"You know who we're dealing with, so don't let your guard down and don't let him out of your sight," Joe reiterated.

"Excuse me, Lieutenant, Doctor Forrest is here."

"Thank you, Sharon, send him in."

Joe remained at his desk but motioned for Robert to join him.

"I thought I'd stop by and see what was going on, I hope I'm not interrupting anything."

"Have a seat, we have Pierce under surveillance and we're hoping to take him without a fight. He's certainly an active person."

"Do you know where Donna is?"

"Not yet."

"Do you mind if I listen in?"

"Can I help you," the waiter asked as he approached Montahue and Brown carrying a pot of hot coffee.

"Two coffees."

As the waiter filled their two cups, Montahue glanced back at Pierce who was now on his feet and putting money on the table. He quickly headed toward the exit.

"Brown, take care of the coffee," Montahue ordered as he hightailed it after Pierce.

"Pierce is on the move; he just left the restaurant and is heading toward the Men's room. He's going inside, and if there is no one else in there, this might be a good time to take him," he whispered discretely into his pen radio.

Pierce quickly scanned the Men's room, two men were standing at the urinals and two of the five stalls were occupied. Pierce removed his hat and coat and hung them on the rack, along with his umbrella. He hastened to an empty stall just as the men at the urinals were leaving. He stepped inside and removed his trousers and put them inside the duffle bag. Then he removed a pair of tan slacks from the duffle bag and put them on. A toilet flushed and he could see a man exiting the stall next to him. The man walked over to the sink and began washing his hands, and as he did he kept eyeing Pierces clothing on the rack. When the timing was right, he threw the paper towel into the sink and removed Pierces' hat, umbrella, and raincoat from the coat rack and quickly left the men's room.

"Follow him inside," Joe ordered.

"Brown, wait here I'm going inside," Montahue said.

As Montahue was entering the Men's room, the man who had just stolen Pierces' clothing was exiting.

Montahue whispered into his pen radio, "A man fitting Pierces description is leaving the Men's room, keep him under surveillance while I check inside."

"We see him," Slater replied.

Other than the two occupied stalls, the men's room was empty.

"We have two in the john, and one is wearing dark slacks but I have no idea whether it's Pierce or not," Montahue reported.

"Montehue, you and Brown position yourselves so that if the man in the dark slacks exits you can take him. If the one in the tan slacks exits first and it's obviously not him, let him go. Slater, keep an eye on the man that just left. Be on your toes and be ready for anything."

"Okay guys, you heard Joe, let's keep him in sight," Slater instructed.

Brown joined Montahue inside the Men's room just as a toilet was being flushed and a man in his mid-fifties was exiting one of the stalls. He was approximately six feet tall, with long blond hair pulled back into a ponytail. He was wearing a cream-colored waist length jacket, a cream-colored turtleneck ski sweater and tan slacks; he had a cane and was limping badly.

"How's it going?" he asked as he carefully and painfully made his way toward the sink.

"Could be better," Montahue replied, "What's wrong with the leg?

The man chuckled, "Stupid me, I broke my leg, hurts like Hell," he said raising his pant leg. He wore no bandage but Montehue could see the two metal braces that held his leg in alignment and a stainless steel pin protruding from his bruised and swollen leg.

"Yeah, I bet it does," Montahue winced. After the man had hobbled from the bathroom, Montehue contacted Joe. "The guy with the tan slacks is a cripple, no way he's Pierce. We're going to take the other guy."

"Be careful," Joe warned.

Montahue unleashed his revolver and positioned himself on one side of the stall while Brown positioned himself on the other. The toilet flushed, and with guns pointed squarely at the door, they lay in-wait. When the door opened, Montahue and Brown both shouted, "Freeze you're under arrest." The man grabbed his heart and slumped backward landing in the middle of the toilet. He was not only elderly, but also obese.

"Make sure he's all right," Montahue ordered as he activated his pen radio, "Joe, this isn't him, Slater must be following Pierce."

"Joe, the man with the overcoat and umbrella is in the parking lot and there isn't anyone else around, maybe this is a good time to take him." Slater proposed.

"Okay," Joe confirmed, "let's close in."

"Hold on, it looks like he's trying to break into a car. He is, he's breaking into a car," Slater announced.

"What the Hell's going on?" Joe snapped. "Montahue, find the cripple, he's our guy!"

The detectives made an immediate sweep of the hotel, searching every conceivable place he might hide, but he appeared to have vanished into thin air.

Montahue returned to the men's room, it was empty but sitting on top of the toilet used by the cripple sat a red duffle bag containing one pair of dark slacks and a note that read in bold letters, IMBECILES!

"Shit Joe, it was him and I lost him," he said snatching up the duffle bag.

"Okay everybody, it looks like he made us," the tone in Joe's voice indicating how important the loss was.

"Now what?" Robert asked.

"I'm going to personally camp out on his doorstep and wait for him to show up," Joe countered.

"Do you mind if I go with you?"

"Do you think that's a good idea?"

"Maybe not, but he does have my wife and I won't get in your way," he promised.

Joe nodded, knowing Robert had more to lose than anyone. "Okay," he said picking up his thermos, "fill this with hot coffee, it may be a long night."

Robert nodded, "Thanks."

Joe positioned his car so that he could see the road leading up to Pierces' house.

"Well, this is where the fun begins," he said looking at Robert. "You've gone through a lot, and I want you to know I'll do everything in my power to get Donna back safely."

"I know you will," Robert replied, his voice cracking and his eyes turning misty. "I just don't know what I'd do if anything should happen to that girl."

"Nothing's going to happen, he's clever but it's him against all of us. How about some of that coffee?" Joe asked changing the subject.

Robert looked at Joe without answering, "How can you do this, I mean just sit and wait?"

"It takes years of practice to do it right," he chuckled. "I remember one of my first stakeouts; we sat in the attic of a Seven Eleven store for four straight weekends. Now I'm talking from eight in the evening until two in the morning, anyway the week's drug by until finally the robbery suspect's came in. One held a shotgun on the cashier, a young college girl, while his compadre jumped over the counter and took the money from the register. It was too dangerous to take them inside, so we were forced to sit and watch while they robbed the store. Our plan was to take them outside, that is until one put his shotgun to the girl's head and began threatening to shoot her. She flipped out, and he became so nervous I was afraid he was going to kill her. I had no choice; I hit him in the head. I can still hear the thud as the bullet struck his skull. The other suspect panicked, he didn't know where the shot came from so he turned his gun on the girl thinking she did it. My partner got him, the poor girl escaped unscathed but she was scared to death."

"That's brutal," Robert responded.

"Life's brutal," Joe replied calmly. "You wait and wait, and when it finally goes down it happens so fast you don't have time to think, only react as you've been trained." Joe paused, "How about that coffee?"

Robert smiled and began pouring the coffee, "I'm glad I have someone like you when Donna's life is on the line."

Joe continued as if not hearing Robert's comment. "The hardest part of a stakeout is constantly reminding yourself why you're there, and being ready at a moments notice."

"Yes sir, I get the message," Robert answered bringing his full attention back to Pierces' house.

They sat in the shadows under cold and gloomy skies as the hour's drug by until their hopes faded like a falling star. Joe looked at his watch, Ten-thirty PM. "We haven't eaten all day and it looks like he's going to be a no show, shall I call for replacements?"

Robert began massaging his temples, "We know he's had several residences, I guess there's no reason to believe he doesn't have another. You will call me if anything happens?"

Without answering, Joe picked up the mic, "Six-W-Three, this is Six-W-Ten."

"Go ahead, Joe."

"Hold on, Joe, there's a car coming."

"Six-W-Three hold on."

The car crept up the street without lights, and when it reached Pierces' driveway it stopped in the middle of the road. It sat there for a few moments, and then it turned into the driveway and parked in front of the house. The drivers' door opened and Pierce stepped out, he scanned the area and then quickly ran into the house.

"Damn, I was hoping to get him before he got into his house. Six-W-Three come in."

"Yeah Joe, go ahead."

"Pierce has returned, but Donna wasn't with him. What's your prognosis?"

"Two Black and Whites are just below Pierces' house, and I'm just around the corner from your location with two more."

"Donna must to be in the house, so we…hold on Pierce just came out, let's get him before he gets back inside. Everybody move!" Joe ordered.

Joe put peddle to the medal, and with tires squealing and rubber burning the car shot forward like a cannon.

Pierce saw the car racing toward him, but for some unknown reason he waited until it came to a screeching halt only a few feet away before turning to run.

"Police, you're under arrest," Joe shouted to no avail. He and Robert gave chase but Pierce moved with the quickness of a fullback, running into the master bedroom and bolting the double doors.

"Damn, we almost had him," Joe commented, frustrated because it seemed they were always two steps behind.

Joe began pounding on the double doors, "Pierce, we have a warrant for your arrest. Your house is completely surrounded and you cannot possibly escape, give yourself up."

There was no response.

"Okay, you leave us no choice," Joe warned.

Joe thrust his shoulder against the barrier, but the doors held like a fortress, "We'll never break through these doors," he commented.

"We'll wait for the others, he's not going anywhere."

Then a peculiar scent struck Joe's nostrils, "Gasoline, it's a trap." But before they could react….Ka-boom went one blast, Ka-boom went another, then in rapid succession the others exploded, blowing fire and burning debris throughout the house. The blast lifted Joe and Robert off their feet and threw them against the wall some distance away.

Robert landed on his back, his face was bleeding profusely from cuts caused by flying fragments of glass and debris, his coat was on fire and he could feel the intense heat of the flames. He took his coat off and threw it aside.

Joe was knocked semi-unconscious and was bleeding profusely from his nose and both ears. He was lying on his back under a fallen bookcase, "Joe, are you all right?" Robert asked as he removed the bookcase. Joe had sustained a compound fracture of the right leg and his femur bone was protruding through his trousers. "We have to get you out of here," Robert said trying to lift him. "Joe, I can't pick you up, you're too big. If you don't help me, you'll die."

Joe was in shock but still managed to struggle to his feet, and with Robert's assistance they stumbled down the flame-engulfed hallway to the front door and into the arms of two awaiting policemen.

"My wife is still in there," Robert shouted as he turned and raced back inside.

He made it as far as the front room, but the staircase was now completely engulfed in flames and the heat was so intense he had to retreat. As he did, a fire truck was arriving at the scene and two firemen rushed to his side.

"Are you okay?" one asked.

"I'm okay, but my wife's in there."

"I'm sorry, but I can't send anyone in," he replied.

"You can't just leave her in there to die," Robert shouted "I'm going in."

"I can't let you, it's too dangerous."

"You can't stop me," Robert retorted. "Give me your hat and coat."

"I can't do that," the fireman replied.

Robert looked at Joe, his eyes filled with tears, "Lieutenant, please."

"Give him your damn hat and coat, for God's sake." Joe snapped.

The fireman reluctantly removed his hat and coat and handed them to Robert. "You might as well have this, too!" he said handing him his gas mask.

Robert put the hat and coat on, and the fireman shook his head as Robert fumbled clumsily with the gas mask. "That's not the way you wear it," he scolded. "Bring the straps back like this and pull it tight against your face so it won't leak."

Then the fireman drenched a blanket with water and put it over Robert's shoulders for added protection. Robert turned to Joe and Joe gave him the thumbs up. "Go get her," he said.

"I can't believe I'm letting him go in there," the fireman said shaking his head. "He'll die in there."

"Don't worry about him, he'll make it," Joe snorted as Robert reentered the blazing building.

The whole room was now completely engulfed in flames, and was like walking into an inferno. The damage caused by the explosion was so extensive that reaching the second floor was out of the question.

"No..." he cried, knowing that if Donna were on the second floor, it would be impossible for him save her. He had to make a decision, and his only hope was that Pierce had kept her on the first floor. The smoke was so thick he was unable to see his hands in front of his face and he had to literally feel his way down the hallway.

Robert had never been in a situation like this, and his wife's life depended on him finding her expeditiously. To make matters worse, he had to do it in a place he was completely unfamiliar with, and if that wasn't enough, he had to do it while in a state of blindness while a raging fire was devouring everything in its path.

He found the first bedroom without incident, it was empty but it cost him precious time and he could not afford to lose any more. He continued down the hallway until he found another opening. It was another bedroom, but in the midst of the confusion he tripped over a small table and stumbled, striking his gasmask against one of the bed posts. The fall dislodged his gasmask and hot smoke filled his lungs, followed by an irritation of the eyes of catastrophic proportions. Clinging to the bed-post for stability, he began searching the bed in hopes of finding his gas mask, but instead he found what appeared to be a woman's body.

In near panic, he ran his fingers over the curvature of the face in an effort to determine whether it was Donna, or merely a Donna-doll like the one Joe had shown him earlier. He could not tell which he held in his arms. Time was of the essence, and if it were Donna he would never let anything happen to her again, on the other hand if she were merely a Donna-doll, he would have to live the rest of his life in torment knowing she died because he failed to keep his promise to her.

Without the protection of the mask, the intensity of the smoke was overwhelming and he choked with every breath. He removed the blanket from his shoulders and wrapped it around the woman's limp body. He picked her up and stumbled toward the door just as a large chunk of burning embers fell from the ceiling, igniting the bed. Smoke inhalation and exhaustion was rapidly taking its toll, and the extra weight he was carrying only added to his predicament. He tried side-stepping burning debris lying in his path, but lost his balance and stumbled to the floor. He knew he could not continue much farther, but he also knew if he gave up they would both die. He didn't know where the reserve energy came from, or if someone or something was giving him a helping hand, but somehow he managed to struggle to his feet and continue in what direction he did not know.

He saw the timber falling, but it was too late; he turned taking the brunt of its force on his left shoulder. Flames raced across his back and his nostrils caught the scent of burning flesh, then came the excruciating pain in his right leg as an ember lodged itself deep within. His leg buckled and he stumbled to the floor. He tried to rise, but he was spent and fell backwards. It was over; he could not go any farther. "Oh God, please don't let her die like this," he pleaded. Suddenly a gush of cold water drenched them both.

We interrupt our scheduled program to bring you news of a raging fire that's presently burning out of control in the secluded area of the Hollywood Hills. Hello, I'm Troy George, and our very own Virgil Thomas is at the scene."

The cameras switched from Troy George in the KNXT studio to the location of the raging fire, giving their viewers a panoramic view. Several fire trucks were at the front of a large bricked mansion and dozens of firemen were battling a fire whose flames were shooting high above the rooftop. Police were securing the perimeter, not only to keep the curious spectators out of harms way, but also in an effort to capture a murder suspect should he be fortunate enough to escape the raging fire.

"Virgil, can you tell us what's happening and have they found the cause for this horrendous fire?"

"Troy, the fire started inside the residence shortly after Ten-thirty this evening. We've interviewed several neighbors and they say just prior to the fire several loud explosions were heard coming from within the mansion. When they looked out their window, several police cars were already at the scene. We are trying to contact a spokesman for the police department in hopes of attaining more formation in regards to this information, and we'll be bringing you an up-date as soon as we do."

"Do you know whose residence it is?"

"Yes Troy, the neighbors tell us it belongs to a Doctor Stanley Morgan, and although he's lived here for quite some time, it seems they know very little about the man. Neighbors say he's gone most of the time and when he is home he's somewhat of a recluse. As strange as it sounds, no one has ever actually talked with Dr.

Morgan, and they have absolutely no personal information about the man."

"Do you have any information as to whether Dr. Morgan or anyone else might be inside at this time?"

"No Troy, no one seems to know the answer to that question."

"Thank you, Virgil. That was Virgil Thomas of KNXT television, bringing us a live up-date."

"Troy, I'm just now receiving information that Captain Murdock of the Hollywood Special Task Force has arrived and is preparing to make a formal statement."

"Virgil, while we're anxiously waiting Captain Murdock's statement, let us go to the rear of the mansion where Peter Martin is standing by. Peter, can you hear me?"

"Yes Troy, I hear you."

"What do you see at your location?"

"Troy, this is the biggest residential fire that I've ever encountered, flames can be seen shooting twenty feet above the rooftop of the second floor. The pressure inside is so great that numerous windows have blown out, and glass and debris can be found only a short distance from where I am now standing. Firemen are throwing everything they have at the blazing fire, but it is burning so hot the water only dissipates. Police have the area completely surrounded and are trying to keep the gawkers at bay. Troy, as luck may have it, here comes a fireman now, maybe I can get a statement. Excuse me, Captain, would you mind answering a few questions?"

"I'm sorry, but I'm really in a hurry."

"Believe me, I do understand, but if you would give our viewers just a moment of your time," he pleaded.

"I'll do what I can, but only for moment."

"Troy, with me is Captain Holmes of the Los Angeles Fire Department. Captain, do you have any idea how this fire may have started?"

"Apparently several explosions occurred inside the residence, and the speed in which the fire spread indicates something was used to help disperse it. We'll have to wait until our investigators file their reports to find out exactly what was used and where it was ignited. I only pray those inside survive."

"Are you implying there were people inside?"

"There were at least two policemen and one woman inside, I have no further information at this time and I really must go."

"Thank you very much, Captain. We now know there may have been at least three people inside the residence at the time of the explosion, and we'll keep you informed as information comes in. This is Peter Martin, reporting live from twenty-six forty-three Robin Hood Lane."

"Thank you, Peter. We now take you back to the front of the mansion where Virgil Thomas is with Captain Murdock of the Hollywood Special Task Force. Virgil, are you there?"

"Yes Troy, I am. Captain Murdock, we've received information that two policemen and one woman may have been inside the residence at the time of the explosion, do you have any information regarding this, and what connection does the Special Task Force have with this fire?"

"I can say this; this is not a normal residential fire. There has been an on-going comprehensive investigation regarding the owner this residence, Doctor Stanley Morgan alias Doctor Edward Bryant Pierce."

"And is this the same Doctor Edward Pierce whose grave was exhumed by Lieutenant Norris recently?"

"The one and same," Murdock replied.

"Can you explain what the police were doing here?"

"When we had gathered sufficient evidence for a conviction for murder against Doctor Pierce, we initiated a stakeout of his residence. We were in hopes of initiating a peaceful arrest and bring the murderer of Barry Snider and five other victims to justice."

"What do you know about the possibility of two policemen and one woman being inside?"

Murdock lowered his eyes sadly, "One of my top investigators, a person whom I admire very much was injured in the blast along with our psychiatrist and his wife. All three have been transported to the emergency room at Sierra View Hospital, and at this time I do not know the extent of their injuries."

"Thank you, Captain Murdock. It appears that the investigation of the serial killer has temporarily come to an abrupt halt, but here at the scene of this horrendous fire, there is no sign of backing off. As I look around the area, I see dozens of firefighters trying to stop the unstoppable, and I pray that the lives of the three are not in jeopardy. This is Virgil Thomas, KNXT television; live from twenty-six-forty-three Robin Hood Lane."

"Thank you, Virgil, for that comprehensive report and we will keep you informed as the story unfolds. This is Troy George, good-night."

Robert was unaware of the circumstances surrounding his rescue; he only knew an angel was standing over him.

"Is my wife…"

"Shhh," the nurse said placing her finger over his mouth, "your wife is fine," and those were the last words he heard as he left the world of the conscious, but this time there was a smile on his face.

Chapter Seventeen

Robert pushed the door open and peered inside; Joe was lying in bed with his right leg in a cast up to his waist and elevated by a strap connected to the metal frame. It was lunch hour and a food tray straddled Joe's chest and Cole was in the process of scolding him for not eating his broccoli.

"I hope I'm not interrupting a dietary squabble," Robert called out trying not to laugh and break any of the stitches in his cheeks or lips.

"Hey Bob, you're a doctor, what's your opinion of broccoli?"

"I think you're not a very good patient."

"If the President of the United States doesn't have to eat broccoli, why should I?"

"See what I have to put up with. If you're going to stay healthy, you have to eat your green veggies," she chided, shaking her finger at him.

With the aid of his crutches, Robert limped in and sat down. "Other than a broken leg, he certainly looks healthy to me." Robert chuckled. "But you better eat your broccoli or the little green monster will get you."

Joe began chuckling, "Green monster? How's the leg?"

"Hurts like Hell. How's yours?"

Joe shrugged patting his cast, "They say I won't be dancing for a while."

"That should make you happy, you don't like to dance anyway," Cole injected.

"You're moving pretty well on those things, Doc, don't get a whiplash going over any speed bumps," Joe chuckled.

With a straight face, Robert countered, "I can get rubber in second gear."

Cole began laughing, "Will you two stop before you cause me to rupture something?"

"That food looks pretty enticing, what is it?" Robert asked as he began scrutinizing Joe's plate.

"This is broiled chicken," Joe said poking it with his fork. "And it tastes like fried cardboard. And that green stuff, well you know what that is and I'm not going to eat it."

"Will you two stop it," Cole scolded. "I can see I've spoiled you rotten."

"She is a good cook," Joe confessed.

"I have to go, I just wanted to stop by and make sure you were okay?"

Joe turned serious, "I want to thank you for saving my life."

"And I want to thank you, too," Cole said giving Robert a big hug.

Robert's face turned flush.

"How's Donna?" Cole asked.

"She's doing great, she'll be coming home next week," he said with a sparkle in his eyes. "Oh before I forget, she wanted me to ask how Dot was doing."

"Dot's doing fine," Joe answered. "She stopped by yesterday, said she'd never been so scared in her life as when Pierce put Donna in a wheelchair and took her out of their room. She was so frightened for Donna, and there was nothing she could do to stop him."

"Donna really became fond of her, too. The next time you see her, ask her to call. I know Donna would like that. I've really got to go, but when everyone's out of the hospital, let's throw a party?" Robert suggested.

"Yeah, let's do that," Joe replied.

213

The smoke is so thick in the little neighborhood bar that it is stifling. The music is turned off and every eye is glued to the television set as Mayor Walsh honors Captain Murdock and his team for solving the serial killings. The event is being covered throughout all fifty states by the three major networks and rebroadcast by their affiliate stations. News personalities from both television and radio are packed into a cluster and clambering for center stage. It is their time to shine as a professional journalist, and each is hoping to be the one selected to ask the question that is on the lips of every person who has followed the heinous crimes.

Mayor Walsh, wearing a huge smile, raises his arms as if he were Sir Lancelot and had just slain the mean ole' dragon. "Ladies and gentlemen, we are gathered here on the footsteps of City Hall to report the final closure of the crimes that have been terrorizing every facet of our wonderful city. I would like to personally thank all the police personnel who were involved in this investigation, it has taken a tremendous amount of dedication and investigative ingenuity to capture one of the worst and most senseless killers the City of Los Angeles has ever known. Just knowing they were out there gave me the comforting thought that one day he would be caught and our lives return to normalcy. I want to publicly thank Captain Murdock for heading the Special Task Force. He had already given notice to the City of Los Angeles of his pending retirement, when I had the good fortune to have him visit my office. I asked, and Captain Murdock was gracious enough to postpone his retirement until this assignment was concluded. Mayor Walsh motioned for Captain Murdock to join him at the microphone, and as he did the Mayor shook his hand. "I want to thank you, Captain, and all your officers for a job well done." He then turned to the media, "Now if there are any questions?"

"Mayor...Mayor," they began shouting.

"Okay, okay;" the Mayor chuckled. "Tom, go ahead."

"Thank you, Mayor; Tom Burch of the LA Examiner, we're all aware of the fire that broke out in the home of Doctor Stanley Morgan alias Doctor Edward Pierce, and that a charred body was found at the scene. How can we be absolutely sure that the body found this time was that of Dr. Pierce, when he was the supposed victim of a homicide on April Fourteenth, Nineteen Eighty-four and his body was also supposedly found among the ashes then?"

The Mayor began chuckling, "Tom, that's an excellent question, and I'm glad you asked. However, I think it would be more appropriate if Captain Murdock were to answer it."

Murdock stepped to the mic, "With all due respect, before I answer your question, I'd like to take this opportunity to publicly thank Mayor Walsh for his generous and much needed support during this whole ordeal. I'd also like to take this opportunity to thank a couple of people, without whose help we might still be looking for this murdering SOB, if you'll pardon my expression."

"First, I'd like to thank Lieutenant Joe Norris who went way beyond the call of duty. Secondly, I'd like to thank Doctor Robert Forrest for his professional services during the long months of investigation at the cost of much personal tragedy. Now to answer your question, in Nineteen Eighty-Four police were summoned to investigate the break in and murder of Doctor Edward Bryant Pierce and his wife, Joan Rachel Pierce. The residence was completely burned to the ground and the remains of two persons were found among the ashes. Their bodies were in such a state that dental records had to be used for identification. A death certificate was issued for each victim after his or her identity was verified. But during the investigation of our recent murders, fingerprints were found that revealed Doctor Edward Pierce was in fact still alive. Further investigations revealed that his new identity was that of Doctor Stanley Morgan. When we gathered enough evidence, Lieutenant Norris, accompanied by Doctor Forrest, attempted to arrest him. Unfortunately, Pierce lured them into a trap. Lieutenant Norris is currently in the hospital with a compound fracture of the right leg and Doctor Robert Forrest is limping around on crutches. Dr. Forrest's wife was the victim of a kidnap, and she is now in the hospital recuperating from severe smoke inhalation. Pierces body was burned beyond recognition, but I guarantee you, he has paid the maximum price for his crimes."

The crowd reacted with jubilant applause.

The bartender states to the man sitting at the bar, "The murdering son-of-a-bitch got just what he deserved. Ye know I saw a reporter interviewing a fireman the night of the fire; he could have been your twin brother. Oh by the way, what ever happened to Jake?"

The man smiles as he picks up his Scotch, downing it in one gulp, "Why? Do you miss him?"

"Me miss him? Why I hope that son-of-bitch burns in Hell," he snorted.

The man begins chuckling, a sparkle showing in his steel-gray eyes, "I'm sure he will," he says cheerfully. "Get me another drink."

"Sure thing, Doc."